POWER EXCHANGE

SADIE HALLER

QTP

ISBN: 978-0-9959811-3-3

ABOUT THIS BOOK

Want to hook up with a kinky fellow celebrity near you?
There needs to be an app for that.

I have a quiet reputation for fixing the most sordid and tawdry of situations. Preventing them in the first place? For that, I'm going to need a little help. But what Stuart wants in return...

Fetwrk is a hook-up app for the debauched and kinky
More whips and chains than hearts and flowers

BOOKS BY SADIE HALLER

Dominant Cord

One Gold Heart

One Gold Knot

One Gold Triquetra

Tainted Pearl

Tainted Shadow

Power Brokers

Chief of Perversion

Agent of Denial (Coming soon)

Fetwrk

Power Exchange

Blacklist Hookup

Unfriendly Relations

Frisky Beavers

Prime Minister

Dr. Bad Boy

Full Mountie

Mr. Hat Trick

For whoever needs to be told:
You're beautiful
You're amazing
I love you

PROLOGUE

Mel

1984

It's super late and we've already watched two videos, but I'm not ready to go to sleep just yet. There's a grown-up party going on by the pool, and I want to check it out.

"Let's go peek out the back window," I suggest to Nora, who's been my best friend since we were babies.

"You know we're not supposed to," she protests. "My mom said not to leave my room after bedtime."

"So what? I bet they're all outside busy having fun. Who's going to know?"

"Nobody, maybe. But—"

"Come on," I say, snagging the sleeve of her jammie top.

We sneak out of Nora's room and up to the third-floor

back bedroom where we'll get the best view. Usually, their parties happen down in the big rec-room in the basement where it's impossible for us to spy on them without getting caught. Tonight, though...

We both gasp as we peer out into the back yard.

Naked people *everywhere*, touching and snuggling and—

I know about *that*—sort of. I've walked in on my parents before, we've had *the talk*, and it's definitely been whispered about among my friends. The thing is, I've never seen or heard of people doing it like this.

"We should go back to my room," Nora says, her voice sounding a little panicked. "We shouldn't be watching this. It's bad."

"How is it bad?" I ask. "It looks like everyone is having a good time."

"I don't know. I just have an awful feeling in my tummy, and we should go back to bed and pretend we never saw this."

I'm fascinated by it all and want to keep watching. But Nora's right. Something doesn't quite feel okay, and we don't want to get into any trouble.

"Okay. Let's go."

Just as I turn to leave, something catches my eye in the distance.

ONE

Mel

Present day

Nothing yanks me out of dreamland and slams my brain into fixer-mode like my phone screaming the chorus from The Alarm's *68 Guns*. That ringtone only ever means one thing—some celebrity is neck-deep in the kind of shit that can kill a career faster and messier than a twelve-gauge to the head.

I have a quiet reputation for straightening out even the most sordid and tawdry of situations, and that is only possible because, unlike most public relations consultants —I can't be Googled.

I slide my finger across the screen of my phone, put it on speaker, and start throwing on clothes.

"Seymour."

"Oh, thank Christ. Mel, it's Janet Gilroy calling. Lis Green—she's only gone and found herself an internet Dom, and this time it's a disaster of epic proportions. I don't know how—"

"Calm down. Where is she?"

"Mountain View Day Spa." The official name of the very exclusive medical clinic that fixers like me rely on for clients with medical emergencies requiring absolute discretion.

"And the Dom?"

"No idea."

Fuck. "I'll be there in thirty."

Twenty-three minutes later, I arrive to find Lis Green is an absolute fucking mess.

She's lying face-down on the bed, her body covered with whip slashes from her shoulders down to her calves. If she's lucky, the scars will fade to a point where makeup will hide them well enough for the camera. If not, she's going to require a body-double for skin scenes.

"I get that you're scared and hurting, but I need you to tell me everything you know about this guy."

"I just want it to all go away."

"I know, and the best way for that to happen is for you to give me all the information you can. We've been down a road like this before, so you know I'm very good at what I do."

"But this time..."

It's the first time she's been physically fucked up. "Lis, the sooner I can jump on this, the easier it will be to keep it contained."

"I met him through this BDSM site. It's got some forums and social areas, but it's mostly for hooking up. Profiles include kinks and limits and stuff."

"Do you mean Fetlife?"

"No. I do have a profile there, but no. This one is —underground."

"I'm going to need the URL and this asshole's username."

I pull out my phone and fire a text off to Wil Johnston, my investigator.

Mel: Need you to locate user MasterSteve on domn8.kink ASAP.

Wil: On it.

"They're going to fix you up and let you recuperate here for a few days, and then we'll move you to an exclusive resort until you're fully healed. As far as the world will know, you're just taking a much-needed break."

"Thank you, Mel."

"No problem. Call me if anything comes up. I'll be in touch when I have updates, okay?"

"Okay."

Three hours later, Wil calls.

"I've located the fucker. What do you want me to do?"

"Come get me. I think I'd like to have you there for

this one." I've been at this a long time, and I am pretty good at taking care of myself. But part of that is knowing when to have back up. Given the damage this fucker did to Lis, it's better Wil comes with me.

As it turns out, this asshole isn't much of a challenge. Just like most abusers, he's nothing more than a coward. Wil dug up more than enough dirt on him—activities that can in no way connect him to Lis—that will get turned over to the cops if he violates the terms of the non-disclosure agreement I have him sign. Okay, so it's possible the cops may get an anonymous tip at some point in the not too distant future because oh golly gee, *Wil* didn't sign anything...

If there's one thing I can be sure of, this won't be the last time I bail some celebrity out of trouble for taking a walk on the sexual wild side. Unfortunately, the number of celebs taking that walk is increasing, and as evidenced by Lis, the pedestrians who come back for more are taking bigger and bigger risks with each excursion.

TWO

Stuart

Waking up knowing I have three blissfully free weeks before I need to start my next contract made it well worth staying up until the wee hours of the morning to finish and submit the project that has consumed almost every waking hour for the past six months.

I'm just getting a fresh pot of coffee going when Hayden knocks on the kitchen door.

"Coffee should be ready to go in a few minutes," I tell him as I usher him in. "So, what's up?"

"What makes you think something's up?"

I raise an eyebrow. "How often do you call me during a workday to get together for coffee?"

"Okay, you may have a point."

"So?"

"Fuck. Why is parenting so damned hard?"

"I have no kids. I know nothing about raising them. I

am the last person on the planet you should be asking that question."

"You're her godfather."

"Yes. Which means my job is to spoil her rotten and send her home, and step in for you if— Shit, Hayden, are you—"

"No. I'm fine. She's not losing her other parent anytime soon. I think she's into something hinky online."

"Ah. That sort of thing I *do* know about. You want me to go through her devices?"

"Yeah. But more than that. I want you there when we talk about it. She adores you. She's more likely to be receptive to the realities if they're coming from you than she would from me. And I'd rather have her consent than have to pull the parental authority card when it comes to scrubbing her devices. Again, she'll probably be more cooperative with you."

"I guess this is how I'll be spending my afternoon, then."

"I'll feed you, though. And maybe even ply you with a beer or two."

"Deal."

After Hayden leaves, I do some research and contact a few experts—some in law enforcement, some from the opposite end of the spectrum—and pick their brains before loading up my gear bag and heading out.

My gut is roiling. My place in Ffion's life has always been that of the affable, doting uncle. This afternoon, I have to say goodbye to that role forever. Because the moment I have to be deadly serious with her, our relationship will be irrevocably changed.

I purposely arrive before Ffion is due home from school. I need to get myself into the right headspace, and Hayden and I both feel it's best if we don't give her a chance to settle into her routine.

"Stuart!" She bounds across the living room and I stand just in time to catch her before she lands in my lap.

"Hey Sweetpea."

Her joy doesn't last long as she catches sight of all the equipment I have laid out.

"What's going on?" she asks, warily. Her suspicion adds to my concern.

"Have a seat. We need to have an important discussion."

"Have you been snooping through my things?" she accuses as she looks back and forth between Hayden and me.

"No. Not without your knowledge." Hayden says.

"But you'd do it without my permission."

"I'd prefer we had your permission, but I am your parent, and if I have concerns about your safety and well-being, then it's a battle I will pick."

I take over, because what little calm Hayden has maintained is rapidly swirling the drain.

"Hayden, I'm sure you've probably got some important work you should be getting on with in your office," I say as I flick my gaze toward the door.

"Yeah. No shortage. Let me know when you're done."

As soon as we hear Hayden's office door close, I look at Ffion, wondering how she went from the tiny wee baby I held in my arms to a kid on the cusp of becoming a teenager in barely the blink of an eye.

"Ffion, you're growing up. Way too fast for my liking, and with that comes a lot of exploration. Most of it good, but some of it can be dangerous. There are adults who prey on young people. And they are very good at fooling them into thinking they're someone they're not."

"And because other kids get fooled, you think I'm stupid?" The hurt on her face is an absolute punch to the gut. How do people do this whole parenting gig?

"This has nothing to do with your intelligence. You know I love you, right?"

"Well, yeah."

"Okay, shoe on the other foot for a minute. I know you love me. Would you risk making me upset or maybe even hating you for a while if you had the power to protect me from some bad stuff?"

"I don't know." She drops her chin to her chest.

"Really?" I ask, tipping her chin up with my finger.

"Fine. Yes."

"Are you worried I'm going to see private stuff and tell your dad?"

She nods.

"I'll make you a deal. The only private stuff I will tell your dad about is stuff I truly, in my heart, think he needs to know for your own safety. Is that fair?"

"You won't let him see anything?"

"Not unless I feel like you are unsafe. I promise."

"Okay."

"Is there anything you want to tell me up front? Sites you've been visiting?"

"I don't *want* to, but I will."

"Okay. How do you normally access them?"

"On my phone. Because I always have it with me."

"So, never on your laptop or your tablet? What about your video game console? Do you do online stuff with that?"

"No. Not any of those. Too easy for dad—" She stops short, but I can guess the rest. Too easy for her dad to check up. Her phone, not so much. At least not behind her back.

"I will still go through all your devices, if for no other reason than to ensure there's nothing there that shouldn't be, okay?"

"Yeah."

I start with her phone. As I skim through the chatroom logs, I struggle to contain my rage. Conversations that any adult could see through in an instant, but easily make a young girl feel special. Listened to. Important.

"Sweetpea, I need you to make me a promise, right now."

"You're angry."

"Yes. But not at you. Never at you. I need you to promise me that if you ever, and I mean ever need, need more love, or attention, or *anything*, you'll demand it of your dad and me. If you have a problem, you'll come to one of us. We love you. You can see in our faces that we love you. Can you promise me that?"

"I'm sorry."

"Ffion, you don't need to be sorry. I just need to know that you'll come to the people who love you most whenever you have a need."

"I promise. I didn't think—"

"For what it's worth, there are plenty of pretty smart adults who get fooled online. So, don't think kids have that market cornered."

She gives me a little smile and I turn my attention back to her phone.

By the time I'm finished, I'm disturbed as fuck. Even though Ffion had only accessed questionable sites on her phone, it, along with her laptop and tablet are riddled with spyware.

"Sweetie, we're going to need to talk to your dad about some of this stuff. You know that, right?"

"Yeah."

"Do you want to go get him, or shall I?"

"I'll go."

About ten minutes later she returns with her dad, who looks like he's ready to flay the skin off the fucker who'd been grooming his baby.

"Did you tell him everything?" I ask Ffion.

"Yeah. Better to come clean, right?"

"Always."

Hayden sits on the big armchair, folding Ffion into his arms as he pulls her into his lap. "As much as I really want to take away all your access to the outside world, I won't. Stuart will block the sites you've been on as well as all those that are known problems—not because we don't trust you, but because we don't want to risk your privacy. I want you to let Stuart check your devices weekly to ensure they're clean. Okay?"

"Okay, Daddy."

My heart breaks for just how much Ffion has been messed up by being duped. All I can say is thank fuck Hayden figured out sooner rather than later that there might be a problem.

THREE

Mel

I'm surprised to see Eli Simmons walk into my office. Some Mondays are definitely crazier than others.

"Eli, never thought you'd be in need of my expertise."

"Yeah, well, I fucked up big time."

"Start at the beginning and do not leave *anything* out. If I'm to do my job well, you need to tell me everything, even if it's humiliating. *Especially* if it's humiliating."

"I assume you know about BDSM."

Another one already? Jesus Fucking Christ on a Saint Andrew's Cross.

"Yes, you could say I'm familiar."

"Okay, so I went to a private play party on Friday night. Friend of a friend's house. I met a woman, we were having a good time, so we decided to continue playing. I took her to The Lair."

"The Lair?" I thought I knew every kink club in the city.

"It's what I call the private property I own in Hidden Hills."

"Okay. Carry on."

"She's not someone I'd be interested in dating, but... well, she was definitely someone I thought I'd be interested in playing with occasionally. That is, until I dropped her off at her place this morning."

He stops. "Would you mind if I avail myself of your Keurig over there?" he asks, gesturing to the little coffee station in the back corner of my office.

"Of course not. Let me do it, I could use a cup, myself. How do you like it?"

"Strong and black."

A few minutes later, I return with our jolts of caffeine, settle back in my chair, and wait."

After taking a couple of sips, he continues with his story. "Okay, so before she got out of my car this morning, she informed me that if I didn't get her a good role on a certain upcoming blockbuster production, she was going to sell the story of her weekend at Eli's to the highest bidder."

"So, instead of allowing yourself to be extorted, you contacted your manager. Smart man."

"If I were a smart man, I wouldn't be here right now."

"What's her name?"

"Tara Langston."

The name doesn't ring any bells. Sometimes that's a good thing. Sometimes it's not. "Okay, I think that's pretty much all I need from you, for now, anyway. I want you to lay as low as you can for the next week or so. No play parties, and no kinky shit until I have this mess out of the way. Continue as normal but skip the socializing with anyone you know to be even remotely sexually adventurous, just to be safe. Squeaky. Clean. Got it?"

"Got it. I will be the squeakiest. Thanks, Mel."

"You're welcome. Now get out of here so I can do my job." In most cases, I wouldn't believe the client. But Eli has been around for quite some time, and this is the very first indication I've had that he's got a wild side. So for now, I'm inclined to give him the benefit of the doubt.

Two hours later, I'm standing outside Tara Langston's bungalow, ringing the bell.

Minutes later, the door opens to reveal a tall, willowy bottle blonde with large breasts that automatically draw your eye. "Yes?"

"Tara Langston?" I ask, knowing full well she is the woman I'm here to deal with. Thanks to Wil, my investigator, I've seen a number of photos, not all of them flattering.

"Yes. And you are?"

"Mel Seymour. I have a private matter to discuss. May I come in, or would you prefer to conduct our business here on your stoop?"

She opens the door wider and ushers me into a small, drab living room. Not waiting for an invitation, I push aside a jumble of clothes, sit in the cleared space on the sofa, and cut straight to the chase. "I'm here about your attempt to extort Eli Simmons this morning."

She has the decency to at least *look* appalled and a little guilty, but she's an actress, so it's more likely she's disguising her shock and disappointment at her career advancement plan being thwarted.

"Look, here's the deal. You will never so much as hint that you've had an intimate encounter with Mr. Simmons. Ever. Not even to your cronies in the old folks' home fifty years from now. You will never contact him again. If, in the unlikely event you are ever on the same production—and believe me, steps will be taken to ensure that doesn't happen—you will go out of your way to avoid him."

"And if I don't?"

Ah yes, there it is. That edge of defiance. The toe in the water to see just how serious this is.

"Then you can kiss your fledgling acting career good-bye. I only need to whisper a few words in the right ears, and you'll be lucky if you can get a job as a fluffer on a third-rate porn film. The choice is entirely yours."

"I'll consider it."

"You've got exactly five minutes to make your decision and sign this non-disclosure agreement." I pull two copies of the document and a pen from my briefcase and slide them across the coffee table. "If I walk out that door without your full cooperation, all bets are off."

Leaning back in my seat, I set the timer app on my phone for five minutes and watch the many expressions of indecision flit across her features.

She waits until the last thirty seconds to pick up a

copy of the NDA and start reading. She's not even flipped to the second page when my phone beeps.

"Time's up. Sign it right now, or I'm out the door and you take your chances."

"But I haven't finished reading it."

"Not my problem. You sat there staring me down for four and a half minutes instead using that time to read the agreement. That's on you." I'm done with this game of chicken. As I lean forward to retrieve the agreements, she snatches up the pen, hastily signs the copy she'd been holding, and then the one on the table.

When she passes them back to me, I sign both, return one copy to my briefcase, and leave the other on the table. "You can keep the pen." I stand up to leave. "Oh, and you would be wise to read it through *very* carefully. You wouldn't want to inadvertently violate any of the terms. It would be a very big mistake to think pleading ignorance will protect you."

I don't have a good feeling about her at all. I hope I'm wrong, but I'm an excellent judge of character, which is, in part, what makes me very, very good at my job.

When I get to my car, I call Wil.

"Johnston."

"Tara Langston. She signed that NDA, but I don't trust her to hold to it. Keep someone on her for the next month. Then we'll re-evaluate the situation."

"Will do."

My next call is to Eli's manager. It goes to voice mail. "David, It's Mel. It looks like that issue is taken care of, but I want to give it a little more time before I'm sure. Call me if you need me to clarify anything."

I won't call Eli until next week at the earliest. It'll do him good to spend some time worrying about whether his career is going to fall down around his ears. Spoiler alert —it won't. But even if everything got out, he'd still be flying high. He's a man, and the standards are different.

Yesterday, I'd only been musing about perhaps having some lower-risk way to connect people like Lis and Eli with each other. Now, after dealing with two incidents in as many days, it's clear to me there's a real need for something like that, and making it happen just moved to the top of my priority list.

FOUR

Stuart

Two weeks later

My first reaction was to reject the project out of hand. I have more work than I have time and energy for, and I am in the enviable position of being able to pick and choose which projects I want to take on.

The majority are either directly for governmental departments, or government contractors. I prefer these because they tend to be large, interesting projects that pay exceptionally well.

It's not often I get approached by a private citizen for a job, particularly one that is so cloak and dagger—a signed non-disclosure agreement and an in-person meeting before this Mel guy will give me any details. It was those demands that made me want to politely decline, but they also piqued my interest. So, I decided this guy at least merited the courtesy of a Google search.

Plenty of Mel Seymours but none seemed likely to be this one. Could it be an alias?

In the end, curiosity got the better of me. Why not sign the NDA and take the meeting? I can still decline the project if it's not my cup of tea, and in the meantime, I'll have answers.

FIVE

Mel

Given the nature of the business I am about to conduct, I'd expect to be meeting my potential contractor in a downtown skyscraper with a security checkpoint in the lobby. Instead, I'm pulling up in front of a residence in the heart of one of Vancouver's older neighborhoods. So, I fully expect to be greeted by a haggard middle-aged mom who'll lead me to a script-kiddie madly tapping away on a keyboard deep the bowels of the large character home.

Instead, the door is answered by a mountain of a man wearing faded jeans and a black t-shirt that's just tight enough to reveal the contour of his muscles without flaunting them. I look way up, past the nicely trimmed salt and pepper Aragorn beard and into the most beautiful bespectacled green eyes.

Okay, I guess the script-kiddie lives in hot dad's basement.

"You must be Mel."

Nodding, I shake his outstretched hand. "Yes."

"Stuart Cole. Nice to meet you. Come on in. Can I get you something to drink? Coffee? Tea? Water?"

Out of habit, I snatch a quick peek at his left hand, and remind myself that I'm here in a professional capacity. Even if he is single, he's off limits for that reason alone. Besides, while sexy as fuck, he's not exactly radiating the alpha vibe that normally gets my juices flowing.

"No, thank you." I surreptitiously wipe my now sweaty palms on my thighs, grateful I went with the black trousers today. I don't know why I'm suddenly nervous.

He leads me into a large, bright room just to the left of the front door. I've been in countless houses like this, most of which are decorated to within an inch of their lives for the sole purpose of showing off. This is nothing of the sort. It's clearly a home meant to be lived in.

There is a large Persian rug in the middle of the hardwood floor. Both are well worn, but not worn out. Comfortable.

"Have a seat," he says, gesturing to a pair of overstuffed leather wingback chairs near the window. Once I'm settled, he sinks into the other seat, crossing his legs as he leans back. "So, what's so secret we couldn't do this over the phone or video-chat?"

Even though he's signed an iron-clad non-disclosure agreement, and I know he's done secret work for government agencies, I didn't want any risk of leaks. Besides, I prefer to conduct initial interviews with people I intend to do business with in person before signing the contract. I need a chance for that final assessment—it's harder for people to hide who they are inside when they're right there in front of you.

"I need an app."

He cocks an eyebrow, and I commend him for not actually rolling his eyes as embarrassment radiates up my neck. "I suppose I should give you a little background. My job is to get celebrities out of potentially career-ending situations. More and more, those situations have been due to a combination of spectacularly bad judgement and a distinct lack of safe options. And even with my truly exceptional staff, I'm struggling to keep up. What I'm looking for is an app along the lines of Tinder, except for people with very public lives who can't afford to indulge their particular *tastes* outside their own socio-economic demographic."

SIX

Stuart

At my age, I should really know better than to make assumptions.

But, I did.

So, when I opened the door to the most stunning strawberry blonde woman, instead of a middle-aged guy with a pot belly and a severely receding hairline, I nearly swallowed my tongue.

From the momentary look of surprise that flitted across her face before she could rein it in, I guess I wasn't exactly what she was expecting either.

And I'll admit, at first, I had to work at keeping my focus entirely on business, because my attraction to her was distracting as fuck.

At least until she explained the nature of her project. Now, I have zero problem returning to my strictly professional self, because I'm actually kind of offended.

I'm all for making an honest buck, and it can be highly lucrative to provide what the paying public wants.

But that's just not me.

I pride myself in only participating in projects I consider to be of a practical nature.

Judgmental? Sure. But I'm an app snob.

"So, let me see if I understand this correctly. You want me to build you a super-secret hook-up app for people who have everything." I mentally pat myself on the back for keeping the contempt I feel from my expression and my tone. "Why come to me?" I ask.

"Because, like me, you have a quiet reputation."

And I've officially moved well past offended.

A large proportion of my contracts are top secret, and it concerns me deeply to hear I have a reputation outside of governmental agencies and certain large corporations—quiet or otherwise.

While it's true my business is derived entirely through word of mouth, I didn't expect any of those mouths would have the ear of a glorified nanny to the rich and famous.

"I'm sorry, Ms. Seymour, but I'm afraid I can't help you. I will, however, be happy to recommend any number of talented and willing designers to take on your project."

"I don't want any other talented and willing designers. I want the best, and my sources tell me, that's you."

"I appreciate the flattery, but this project is not for me. My time and energy are limited, and I'm not interested in spending either on developing a frivolous app so a bunch of entitled, over-indulged social elites can get their kink on."

"Okay, when you put it like that..."

I try and soften my rejection. "I'm sorry, Mel. This project just isn't a good fit for me. Like I said, I'm happy to suggest others to help you—"

"No, no. It's fine, I understand. I appreciate you taking the time, and on second thought, I would like those recommendations."

"I will email them to you right away."

As she gets up to leave, it occurs to me that we don't have a professional relationship, and I could ask her out. It also occurs to me that I just turned her project down flat, and she may be feeling a little stung.

SEVEN

Mel

That evening, after a long, hot, bubble bath which failed to soak away the day's frustrations, I pull into the nearly full parking lot at Silver, a local BDSM club that caters to kinksters over a certain age.

With any luck, I may even hook up with a Dom who'll take me out of my head for a while. God, how long has it been since that's happened?

I don't get many opportunities to safely hit the kink-club scene, so I take advantage whenever I can. Silver is one of only three clubs I feel safe enough to attend and hold a membership to. The other two are in London and New York City.

I recognize a few vehicles, and I'm content in the knowledge that even if I don't connect with a Dom to play with tonight, there will be some excellent scenes to watch, and a chance to catch up with some friends.

Almost immediately after I enter the main play space, Mitch grabs me into a big bear-hug. A hug I sorely needed.

"Mel, how are you? It's been forever since you've been here."

"Busy, but well. And you?"

"I'm same as always."

Which means, he's still single and sub-less. We've played together once or twice over the years, but it was more therapeutic than anything. No real connection. That said, he's a great Dom, and I wish someone amazing would come into his life.

"Are you playing tonight?"

"No, I'm orientating a couple of new members. Which is why I'm lurking here."

"I'll see you around, then."

"Enjoy your evening, Mel."

Nodding, I turn towards the bar to get something cool to drink but am waylaid by Angie and her husband Tim.

"Hey Mel, great to see you. Are you playing tonight?" Angie gives me a big hug. Yeah. This is why I came. To physically connect with people I like. People who are *what you see is what you get.*

Before I can turn back toward the bar, a scene near the front of the main play area catches my eye and I wander over.

Joel has Heather on a wobble board. Thin rope is attached to her nipples with a set of clover clamps and drawn taut in front of her, while another rope is pulling on her ponytail.

To make matters worse, if she loses her balance, she'll wind up hanging by an anal hook. Well, not exactly. The way Joel has her rigged up, most of her weight would be distributed away from the hook.

Regardless, whichever direction she wobbles, she's in for an unhappy time, but so far, she's holding steady.

"This is too easy for you. Let's make it interesting," Joel says. He holds up an egg vibrator and slides it into her pussy. "Every time the edge of the wobble board touches the floor, you'll get a cane stroke. Color, love?"

"Green, Sir."

She manages to maintain her balance through her first orgasm, but then it all falls apart. Once the edge of the wobble board hits the floor, she'd overcompensate and hit it again, each time earning herself a strike of Joel's cane.

The scene isn't a lengthy one, but I linger longer than most because I love the connection they have. The love Joel has for Heather is obvious in the gentle way he handles her at the end of a scene. I allow myself a little time to live vicariously through the intimate moments these two special people share.

EIGHT

Stuart

The last person I expected to see walk into Silver tonight is Mel Seymour.

In fact, I'd come here with every intention of grabbing myself a willing sub to help me work her out of my system.

Our meeting this afternoon hadn't ended well. Not that my dick cares.

The corset she's wearing is sexy as fuck. The forest green satin with black lace overlay plunges to a deep vee between her breasts, revealing just a hint of the nipples trapped beneath the fabric.

Nipples I want to release from their confines and torture for our mutual pleasure.

Nipples I want to lick, and suck, and bite, and pinch.

I watch her as she works her way through the room,

stopping to speak with a number of people as she circulates.

Apparently, she's no stranger to Silver.

How is it I've never seen her here before?

I've been a regular for the past three or four years and I'm sure I'd have noticed her if we'd ever been here at the same time.

An irrational wave of jealousy surges through my system as Mitch pulls her into a long hug. I have no claim over her, and Mitch is a stand-up guy. He's the club mentor. The guy who takes care of all the newbies looking for help. But none of that matters—the green-eyed monster grabs me by the dick, anyway, because Mitch is a sub favorite, and *very* unattached.

And I feel utterly ridiculous when, not five minutes later, Mel wanders off to chat with Angie and Tim. A sweet couple who are relatively new to the club—and the scene.

Watching her from the fringes makes me feel like a bit of a creeper, but I can't help myself. I want her, but I also don't want to interfere.

I stand at the back of the small crowd watching Joel torture Heather in the most delicious ways, but my attention is focused entirely on Mel.

At the end of the scene, when the crowd begins to disperse, I sidle up just behind her.

NINE

Mel

"Ms. Seymour." Warm breath brushes over my skin, sending shivers through my body before my brain registers the owner of that sinfully deep voice. "Are you here for business or pleasure?"

Pleasure. Most definitely pleasure.

But not with him, no matter how much my body is begging me, because if there's one thing I never do, is mix pleasure with business. Not that he and I actually *have* any business. "This is a surprise." I keep my tone as neutral as I can.

"A pleasant one."

"Stuart, this can't happen." I gesture back and forth between us.

"Why not? Because we almost had a business connection? I would think someone in your line of work would be very adept at keeping your work and private lives separate."

"I am. By never allowing them to touch in the first place." And coming here was a mistake. I'd hoped to blow off some stress after our meeting this afternoon. Instead, my chest is even tighter, and my shoulders are practically grazing the bottom of my earlobes. "I think I'm going to call it a night. Turns out this isn't what I needed after all. I should finish researching those recommendations you gave me, anyway."

"Sorry I couldn't help."

Couldn't, my fucking ass. *Wouldn't*.

I'm pissed at myself for making the grave error of putting all my faith in one person. I know better. But all my sources told me Stuart Cole is the best of the best, and I'd counted on piquing his interest enough to climb on board the project.

As I'm turning to go, he gently touches my shoulder. "It's obvious to me that you need some relief. I'd like to help with that, if you'll let me."

Tempting, but... "What if we're not kink-compatible?"

"That's what negotiations are for." He says it with a lopsided grin that goes a long way to melting my resolve. "Let's get something to drink and have a discussion. If it turns out we don't have enough common ground, then I'll set you up with a more suitable play partner. Sound fair?"

"Just so we're clear, if I don't think your kinks mesh closely enough to mine, you'll hunt down a more suitable Dom to take care of me for the evening?

"Absolutely."

I study his face carefully and find not even the slightest sign that he's not being straight up with me. "Then I guess we negotiate."

TEN

Stuart

What the fuck was I thinking? Find her another Dom?

She was about to walk out the door, and the words spewed out of my mouth before my brain could call them back.

I lead Mel to an unoccupied table. "Have a seat, and I'll grab us some water, unless you want something else?"

"Water's great, thanks."

While I'm at the bar, I pick up a couple of limit lists and pencils. One of the best things about Silver is how easy they make negotiations.

"Here you go," I say as I place Mel's water, pencil, and list on the table in front of her. "You fill out yours while I fill out mine, and when we're done, we'll compare notes."

Nodding, she picks up the pencil and gets to work. I watch her for a moment, noting how quickly she moves through the questionnaire, and start in on my own set of limits.

The list the club uses is a bit on the short and simple side, but it's good enough for negotiating casual play in a public setting.

I've completed so many of these over the years, I could almost do it in my sleep. Or just make copies and keep them handy.

While I wait for Mel to finish up, I take the opportunity to really study her in a way that would have been entirely inappropriate in our meeting this afternoon.

She's got that classic, timeless beauty. Her long, strawberry blonde braid is flecked with gray. Her skin has a porcelain translucence that I hope will bear my marks by the end of the evening. I have no doubt the contrast would be spectacular.

As soon as she puts her pencil down and hands her paper over to me, I slide mine across the table to her.

First, I skim through to note the important stuff, searching for anything that clashes with my own hard limits—the stuff I won't do, and the stuff I won't do without.

Nothing jumps out as problematic. In fact, we appear to be surprisingly compatible.

My second time through her list is more thorough, comparing her level of interest for each activity and kink against my own. We're a much closer match than I could have hoped for. And much to my delight, I won't have to find her a more suitable Dom to play with tonight.

"Anything on there that's a significant problem or barrier to you playing with me?" I ask.

"No."

"Is that how you answer a Dom?"

"No, Sir." She blushes, and damn, it's positively adorable.

"Good. In that case, please go use the restroom, because I don't want to have to stop in the middle of a scene because you've got a full bladder." I nod towards her empty glass. "My sadism doesn't stretch quite that far."

"Yes, Sir."

"Good girl."

When she returns a few minutes later, I gesture for her to sit back down on her chair.

"First thing, what's your safeword?"

"Red, Sir. Yellow if I need you to check in."

"Very good. How are you feeling today? Anything sore or tight? Any issues that could affect your flexibility?"

"No, Sir," she says after a slight hesitation.

"Are you sure?" I ask in my best don't fuck with me tone.

"Well, my shoulders are a little tight, but I don't expect that to be a problem."

"Your job is to make sure I have *all* information, so I can assess the situation for myself and avoid any potential problems. Understood?"

"Yes, Sir. I'm sorry."

"Anything in your past that I could accidentally trigger?"

"No, Sir."

"In that case, let's start with some cuffs. Come here." Reaching into my bag, I pull out a set of black leather cuffs and fasten them on her wrists and ankles.

Standing in front of me like she is, her tits are at face level, and I don't deny myself the pleasure of her nipples any longer.

Hooking my index finger into the top edge of her corset, I pull down just enough to reveal one dusky pink nipple. I lean in and graze it gently with my teeth before closing my mouth around it and giving a good, hard suck. Her moan goes straight to my cock. If I'm only going to get one night with her, I'm going to make it fucking legendary.

For both of us.

ELEVEN

Mel

His ability to keep his alphatude from bleeding through his professional facade during our meeting was nothing short of impressive. I know from experience it can be difficult to keep certain parts of one's personality out of business situations—as evidenced this afternoon when I fought against my attraction to him.

An attraction I didn't quite understand until now.

Looks are only part of it for me. A man who can take me in hand and make me submit—make me *want* to submit—that's the stuff of wet panties and happy memories.

And as attractive as I found him earlier, I sure as hell didn't get a Dom vibe off him, let alone evil-fucking-Dom.

And by evil-fucking-Dom, I mean that in the best

possible way. Oh my fucking god. Nipple play is my jam, the rougher the better. And he keeps taking me to the knife-edge of orgasm with every nasty thing he does.

Right now, I'm belly down on a spanking bench. My breasts dangle either side of the main support, with clear plastic tubes held firmly in place by a vacuum pull so strong, they are nearly full of nipple.

And the pain is beyond exquisite.

"I don't think you've got enough suction going on." Reaching between my legs, he spreads my pussy lips and seconds later, the intense stretching pressure on my clit has me teetering on a tightrope between sweet, sweet agony and my safeword.

"Take it for me, Mel. You've got this. It'll all be worth it in the end. I promise."

Soon, the pain from my clit dulls to something akin to a burning ache as the suction stabilizes, but if I were standing, I know I'd be bouncing on my toes.

"What shall we do while we wait for these cups to do their job, I wonder?" He tugs each of the tubes hanging from my nipples, re-igniting the pain. "Your ass is looking sadly neglected. Maybe we should see what makes it dance."

He holds a long plastic ruler out in front of me and I almost laugh. He's going to have to do an awful lot better than that to make me flinch, let alone dance.

His rhythmic taps with the ruler are almost meditative, and if it weren't for all the damned suction tugging at my pink bits, I could almost fall asleep.

"Too boring for you? How about this then?" He asks as he passes a fly swatter in front of my face.

Better, but still not going to make me squirm.

Somewhere in the back of my mind, a little voice warns me not to get complacent, but as time wears on and Stuart continues with what I've come to think of as hitty-lite, I kind of stop paying close attention to the implements he's passing before my eyes.

And that's when fire lights across my ass.

The squeak I can't contain is immediately followed by his deep chuckle.

"There we go. Warmup is definitely over."

He lays stripe after stinging stripe across my ass until I'm sure there can be no unmarked skin left, and then comes a paddle.

Not a limit of any kind, but most definitely an eleven out of ten on the hate-it-scale.

"Where are you at, Mel?"

"I'm green, Sir."

"Are you sure? You don't seem to be having such a good time."

"Not a big fan of the thuddy."

"Good to know," he says on the heels of another deep chuckle.

It's a good thing this is a one-night-only thing, because I could see myself forming a love-hate relationship with that chuckle.

"Deep breath for me, and then let it out slowly."

I inhale, and just as my lungs are at capacity, he

releases the vacuum pressure on all three cups, and my brain is fried as it's unable to discern which pain to process.

A slow exhale is beyond my ability. Instead, I let out a high-pitched screech.

"Oh dear. Not what I told you to do at all, was it?"

"I'm sorry, Sir," I manage between pants.

And there's that chuckle again, followed by a starburst of agony. First on my clit, then my nipples.

"You could have had an orgasm...or maybe even two. Instead, you get clamps and an extended paddling first. Safeword if you need to."

Oh god.

Each thwack he lays across my ass has enough force behind it to make the clamps jiggle, texturing layer upon layer of pain.

This man is entirely merciless.

And I love it.

As my mind takes off to that special place where I have no worries, no cares, the pain morphs to pleasure.

Bliss.

I'm tugged partway out of my reverie when the clamps are removed and blood rushes into my poor tortured pink bits, but the low hum of a vibrator induces a Pavlovian response between my legs just before it slides in and presses up against my g-spot.

"You've been such a good, good girl, Mel. Come as much as you like."

I swear the first orgasm short-circuits my neural pathways, because it's never-ending.

Somewhere in the distance, I hear, "You are so done," followed by that deliciously deep and evil chuckle. And before I know it, I'm swept away, floating on a warm, gentle breeze.

TWELVE

Stuart

She's absolutely perfect.

It's a good thing she's going back to L.A. tomorrow, because I don't know how I'd keep away from her if we lived in the same city.

"Stay right here, I'll be back." I wrap a blanket around her and settle her on the sofa near our play station.

Once I've cleared away my gear and cleaned the equipment, I rejoin her and pull her into my lap.

"You were such a good girl for me. How are you feeling?"

"Loopy."

"Then I've done a good job." I hold a bottle of water to her lips. "Drink."

She takes a few sips, and then I give her a square of chocolate.

A few moments later, she tries to push out of my arms. "I should get going."

"Stop. You need to rest and recuperate. We're not going anywhere until the scene is over, and that includes aftercare. So, relax and let me enjoy what's left our time together."

I pull her tight against me, and she eventually relaxes.

"You were such a good girl, taking everything for me."

"You were evil."

"Did I ever give you any reason to think I wasn't?"

"Yes. This afternoon."

"This afternoon, I wasn't wearing my Dom hat. Just like you weren't wearing your sub hat. All bets were off when you agreed to scene with me. The thing is, I think you like me evil."

"True."

Fuck. Why does she have to be so damned perfect?

"How are you feeling now?"

"Much better. How are you feeling?" she asks as she wiggles her ass against my erection.

"Behave," I warn, hoping she doesn't call my bluff because I don't have the slightest clue how I'd punish her.

"But—"

"I appreciate the thought, but I've got everything I needed." Which is true, though I'd love to take her home with me and ravage every delectable inch of her.

I feel her nod against my chest, and I hug her a little tighter as I fight the urge to kiss the top of her head.

Later, when we're both dressed and have collected

our things, she places her hand on my shoulder and looks up at me.

"Thank you for tonight. I still feel I shouldn't have mixed business with pleasure, but I do appreciate what you've done for me. I should be going, now. I've already been here longer than I'd intended."

"Do you need a ride back to your hotel?"

"No, thank you. I've got a rental outside."

I walk with her to her car.

"You're sure you're okay to drive?"

"Yes, I am. Really."

"Okay. But will you please text me when you're in your hotel room, so I know you are safe?"

"Yes." I cock an eyebrow. "Yes, Sir."

"In that case, thank you for a lovely evening."

Nodding, she gets in her car. I wait until she's buckled in and on her way before jogging through the parking lot to my own vehicle.

THIRTEEN

Stuart

The next morning, as I'm drinking my first cup of coffee and reminiscing over my amazing evening with Mel, the emergency doorbell goes off.

I installed it back when Ffion was old enough to walk herself the two blocks to my house on her own, and it's the one disruption I'm conditioned to respond to, even though she hasn't used it since Hayden got her a phone. The fact that she used the doorbell instead of calling worries me, so I race through the house to the kitchen door.

"Hey Sweetpea." I focus on keeping my voice even and calm, even though the sight of Ffion's blotchy tear-stained face splinters my heart into a million pieces. "Come on in and have a hot drink and some cookies, then you can tell me what this is all about, okay?"

"Okay."

Her backpack hits the floor next to the door with a thud as she toes off her shoes and parks herself in her chair. Because, yeah, she's here enough to have her own spot at the table.

I make hot chocolate with frothy milk, topped with miniature marshmallows, just how she likes it, and place it, along with a package of chocolate chip cookies, on the table as I drop into the chair next to her.

"Thank you."

I let her settle with her drink and snack for a few minutes before I prod.

"Are you going to tell me what's going on?"

"Remember that whole thing where my phone and computer and stuff were all infected and you fixed it?"

"Yes." My heart bangs hard against my ribs.

"It's all back. But I didn't go to any of the sites. I promise. I didn't do anything at all. I swear. That whole thing scared me so bad."

"Is that why you didn't call me?"

"Yeah. My phone is doing weird things. I tried to call dad to come and get me from the library—because I kinda got a lot of books, and my pack is pretty heavy—and every time I tried, it wouldn't connect. Then when I tried to call you, the same thing happened."

I'd hoped that we'd taken care of the issue when I'd sanitized all her devices and had two clear scans since. There was virtually nothing the police could do for us at this point. I did provide them with the details so they could maybe do their own investigation, but I didn't hold out much hope that they'd do anything with the information. Unfortunately, it's one of those angry-making situations where their hands are tied until tragedy strikes.

My mind keeps swinging back to Mel Seymour.

After our meeting yesterday, I'd taken the new information I now had and redid my research. While it's true she's not exactly Google-able, she does leave enough of a professional footprint to get a sense of her, once you know how and where to look.

She's not just a fixer. When it comes to having problems disappear, she is *the* fixer.

And I will promise her whatever frivolous apps her heart desires if she can make this all go away.

"Ffion, I'm going to get this all fixed for you, but I'm going to have to bring in some help, okay?"

"Okay."

"It's going to be fine." As much as I want to make that a promise, I know better. "Sweetpea, I'm going to need all your devices. Gaming console, too. I'll make sure you get all new ones, but these ones will have to be dead to you."

"I understand."

"I'm going to call your dad, get him to bring everything over, and then I'm going to get started on trying to clear this up."

Twenty minutes later Hayden bursts into the kitchen and Ffion runs into his arms. "It's going to be okay. It will. I love you, baby girl."

"Can you make more coffee while I go make a quick call? I may need you two to stick around for a bit."

"Sure thing."

I retreat to my office to make whatever promises necessary to get Mel to help Ffion.

FOURTEEN

Mel

I was just about to settle in for a nice hot bubble bath to soothe some of last night's marks and bruises when Stuart calls.

"Mel, I have a big ask, and I'm willing to do your app in addition to paying for your services."

Not even close to what I expected to hear. "Go on."

"Is there any chance you can come to my place?"

"What's this about, Stuart?"

"My eleven-year-old goddaughter had a problem with an online predator grooming her in a chatroom. I thoroughly cleaned all her devices—they were riddled with spyware, and I thought that was the end of it."

"But it wasn't."

"No. She tried to phone her dad and me this morning, and she couldn't get through. I was hoping maybe you have access to better resources than I do."

"I'll be there as soon as I can." He had me the second he said it was a child in trouble.

"Thank you."

Well, shit. I give my tub full of hot water and bubbles one last longing look before I pull the plug. I call Wil and put him on speaker, throw on some clothes, and pack my gear.

"Hey Mel, how's Hollywood North?"

"I've got something sensitive I'm going to need you to get working on as soon as possible." I give him all the details I have, and the too-long silence makes me think the call had dropped. "Wil?"

"I'm here. Just had to take a minute. I'm going to need everything she has that's ever connected to the internet as well as any chatroom logs and anything else your guy must have downloaded."

My guy. I almost snort. He's most definitely not my guy. "Okay. I'll call you once I have more for you."

"Sounds good. I'll see you later."

It's nearly an hour later by the time I pull up in front of Stuart's house, and he's clearly been waiting on me, because the door is open and he's standing on the porch by the time I'm out of my rental.

"Come on in."

Instead of the left at the front door, Stuart leads me down the hall and into the kitchen at the back of the house.

"Mel, this is my goddaughter, Ffion and her dad, Hayden."

"Nice to meet you, Mel," Hayden says. "Would you like some coffee?"

"I'd love some, thank you."

Stuart pulls out a chair for me and as I sit down, Hayden places a cup of heaven in front of me and points to a sugar bowl and small jug in the middle of the table. "In case you need to doctor it."

"Black is fine, Thank you."

I take a long sip of my coffee and turn my attention to Ffion, who's now sitting in Stuart's lap. His arms are wound tightly around her little body. Every few moments, he kisses the top of her head.

My heart melts.

"Ffion, honey, I'm sorry you're dealing with this. Growing up is hard enough without assholes doing shit like this to make it harder. If you'll let me, I'm going to do what I can to make it all go away."

Her story both splinters my heart and makes me rage-y. And the whole time she's telling it, Stuart continues to soothe her.

When she's done, she hops off Stuart's lap and gives me a big hug.

"It's going to be fine. I promise." And I mean it. Whatever it takes.

She pulls away, studies my face for a minute, and nods.

I shoot a look at Stuart, who just shrugs.

"Do you need us for anything else, Mel?" Hayden asks.

"I don't think so. I'll have my investigator, Wil Johnston, contact you if he needs anything further."

"Thanks. In that case, Ffion, we have some shopping to do. It was nice meeting you, Mel. I hope to see you again soon."

As soon as they leave, Stuart turns his attention all on me.

"With all the crazy this morning I haven't had a chance to ask. How are you feeling?"

"Really good, thank you. I appreciate everything you did for me last night."

"It was my pleasure."

I feel an unreasonable pang of...something I can't define...and I remind myself that right now is business, and I have a plane to catch.

I pull the contracts I had drawn up, in anticipation of Stuart saying yes, out of my briefcase and hand them over.

He reads quickly, then pulls out a pen.

"Don't you want a lawyer to take a look first?" I had zero expectation that he'd go ahead and sign them right away. I was perfectly willing to agree to, him to have his lawyer go over it and fax me the signed contract later.

"No. Everything looks fine. Pretty standard, and considerably less complicated than most contracts I deal with. I assume *you* have a standard contract for retaining your services."

"I do."

"Then why was it not included in this stack of paper?"

"Because this one is on me."

"No."

"Stuart, I don't charge when it comes to kids. I don't care whose kids. When a kid is in trouble, and I can help, I do."

"Yeah, well, when you get the kid I love most in the world out of trouble, you get apps for life." He rips up the contracts and I stare at him, momentarily stunned.

"Now that's taken care of," he says, "when this is over, I—"

"No."

"No? You don't even know what I was going to say."

"You were going to suggest we continue some kind of personal connection once our business is concluded."

"Okay, so you did know what I was going to say, but—"

"It's better that we just leave things as they are. We had a good time and scratched each other's itch." Well, he scratched mine.

"I disagree, but we can table this discussion. For now," he says, raising an eyebrow. And right there, evil-Dom seeps though, soaking my panties. I try not to smile.

"Thank you for taking this on. And thank you again for last night. I do need to be getting to the airport."

Taking my hand, he tugs me towards him, jumbling my insides. "I meant what I said about *for now*. As soon as our business is concluded..." he leaves the sentence hanging, cups my cheek, and kisses me.

It's not hungry and carnal. No, it's sweet and tender, and—dangerous.

I should pull away, but this feels so good, and I just don't want to, no matter how loudly common sense is screaming at me.

When he finally ends the kiss, I'm breathless and aching for more.

"Safe journey, Mel. Please text me when you get home, so I know you've arrived safely."

"Stuart—" I start to protest but stop because I'm being ridiculous. "I will."

He walks me to my car, and stands there, watching until I turn the corner and lose sight of him in my rear-view mirror.

FIFTEEN

Stuart

As soon as Mel leaves, I grab myself more coffee and settle at my desk to start working on this app.

What she's asked for isn't actually that complicated or that much work. It's basically reinventing the wheel. It just needs to be a better, virtually un-hackable wheel.

Realistically, it isn't much more than a high-tech interactive BDSM checklist. A quick Google search, and I come up with a good list to build from. The list Silver uses is good enough for public play, but the majority of people using this app will likely be playing in private.

It is not lost on me that the club actually might benefit from a variation on this. I tuck that thought away for later.

After working most of the day, I order pizza and take it over to Hayden's.

Ffion answers the door and smiles wide when she spots the tell-tale square boxes.

"You're the best, Stuart!" She hugs me around my middle.

"It's been a rough day. I figured this might help a little." We walk through to the kitchen, where Hayden is already pouring me a beer.

"Can I go watch TV while I eat, dad?"

"Sure."

She grabs a plate, loads it with three slices of pizza, and heads off toward the family room.

"How is she doing?" I ask.

Hayden shrugs. "Hard to say. Why is parenting so tough?"

"Because you're doing it all on your own. Have you thought about dating?"

"I can barely find one evening a month to go to the club to let off a little steam, how am I supposed to find the time to date?"

"You know damn good and well I'm more than happy to be the responsible adult so you can have a social life."

"I know. I'm probably just not ready. Now let's talk about something more interesting—Mel, huh?"

Now it's my turn to shrug. "Not if she gets her way."

"Are you going to let her get her way?"

"Not if I can help it."

"Do you think she's really going to be able to fix this?"

I don't hesitate. "Yeah, I do."

"Make sure you let Ffion know that."

Message received. "I'm going to take my pizza and beer and go watch TV with her."

"I'll be there in a few minutes."

Ffion looks up and pauses her show as I walk into the family room.

"Hey, want some company?"

"Sure."

"I feel crappy that I let you down, so I just wanted to make sure you understand that Mel is *really* good at what she does, and I trust her to fix our problem."

"I know. She's really nice. Is she your girlfriend?"

"No."

"But you want her to be?"

"What is it with you and your dad?"

"She's nice. You're nice. Together you'd be twice as nice."

"Start that back up," I say nodding towards the TV. "And eat your pizza."

I stay for another beer, another show, and then head back to my place. I still have a lot of work to do if I'm going to have a mock-up done before Mel gets up in the morning.

SIXTEEN

Mel

Mel: Home safe and sound, and checking in as ordered, Sir.

Stuart: Thank you. How are you feeling?

Mel: A bit tired and achy, but good.

Stuart: Excellent. Text me when you get up in the morning.

Mel: Why?

Stuart: Because I said so.

Mel: Bossy much?

Stuart: Please.

Mel: Fine. How's Ffion?

Stuart: Stressed. Scared. Happier knowing you've got her back. I'm happier knowing that, too.

Mel: I'll text you in the morning as promised.

Stuart: Good girl.

Actually, between Stuart working me over last night and travel fatigue, my body is more than just a little achy, so once I've unpacked, had a bit to eat, and got myself organized for my return to the office tomorrow, I grab some wine and a book and settle in for that nice, long bubble bath I missed out on this morning.

Stuart: Check your email.

Holy shit. He's already got the mock-up ready to go.

I pull up his contact and hit the call icon.

"Thank you for being so quick on this. Do you have any idea when you might have the final version ready to go live?"

"Slow down, Tiger. This kind of thing needs to go through a shit-ton of beta-testing. And that's going to be really hard to do *and* keep it on the down-low, so I'm going to have to give some thought about how to make sure it's ready for primetime without word leaking. My best guess, maybe a couple of months?"

"That's way faster than my best hope, so I'll take it if you can manage it, but I won't hold you to it."

"Why haven't you downloaded it yet?"

"Because I called you instead?"

"Download it and play with it for a while. Sleep on it, and I'll talk to you about it tomorrow, okay?"

"Okay."

As soon as I hang up, I download and install the app on my phone. I laugh my ass off when it immediately pops up with the message that I have met my perfect match.

Mel: I think it's broken.

Stuart: Cheeky. Now go play.

Stuart: Also, let me know when you'll be in town next. I'd like to see you again.

Mel: Not a good idea.

Stuart: It'll be fine. Trust me.

Oh, I want it to be fine. More than I'm willing to admit. But I also know it's better to walk away now. What we did was a mistake. If I'm lucky it's one I'll get away with. And when it comes to luck, I know better than to push it.

I make myself a very big coffee, and settle in with the app.

Of course, I'm feeling feisty, and thankfully, he'd

included plenty of dummy accounts, so I did everything I possibly could to match up with anyone but him.

And failed.

Mel: It's definitely broken. Or rigged. Definitely must be rigged.

Stuart: I dare you to tell me that to my face.

Mel: Not a good idea.

Stuart: We'll talk tomorrow. And a word of advice—don't send any texts your ass can't answer for.

And if that isn't a challenge I kind of want to rise to.

SEVENTEEN

Stuart

It's nearly nine the next morning when I get a call from Mel. Yes, she already has her own special ring tone and alert.

"Hey, how are you doing?"

"I'm fine."

"Any signs of sub-drop?"

"No. All is well. So, the changes I'm looking for—"

"I get that you're feeling all business right now, but I have priorities, and currently, number one my list is how you're feeling." Number two is definitely coffee.

"Sorry. I guess I'm used to getting straight to the point."

"And that's fair, in most circumstances, but I'm going to go out on a limb and assume I'm the only person you're doing business with who's literally gone medieval on your ass. And I think that entitles me to certain privileges, like checking on your well-being."

"Fine."

"And that's not an acceptable answer."

"Stuart, you ceased to be my Dom the minute I got into my car in the parking lot at Silver. And you double-plus ceased to be my Dom when we entered into a business relationship"

"Oh that, I'm afraid, is where you are quite wrong. I will continue to act in the capacity of your Dom for as long as your body bears my marks."

"Stuart—"

"No, this is not negotiable."

"Fine."

"Now, how are you feeling, really?"

"Actually, really good."

"And your marks?"

"Still there."

"Truly no signs of sub-drop, though?"

"I don't think so."

"Have you ever had sub-drop before?"

"Yes. Once."

"Promise you'll call me if you start to feel off."

"Yes."

"Yes, what?"

"Yes, Sir."

"Good. Now, you said you had some changes you wanted to discuss."

"Yes, I really like the safe-call function, but I was wondering if there was some way we could set up something in the back-end. A kind of panic button. Or a ... reverse panic button. Something where the user needs to check in within a certain period of time—which they set themselves—after a hookup. If they don't make it, then we send out some kind of check in message."

"That all sounds very noble, but there is still a very real potential for someone to force an unwilling partici-pant into providing the code."

"What if there were two codes. An I'm fine as well as an I'm not fine code?"

"But everyone knows the rules."

"True, but they would never know for sure which code they've used—Wait. If they're setting their own length of time until check in, they could check in early with a bad-date code. Fuck, I don't know. There's got to be something..."

"I agree. Let me think on it."

"Thank you."

"What other changes were you looking for?"

"I'd like a way to shortlist potential matches. Kind of a maybe option?"

"Interesting. So...Maybe swipe up?"

"Yeah. That would work."

"Anything else?"

"Yeah, I'd like users to also have the option of selecting only people they've played with before or people they've never played with before."

"Okay, so maybe radio buttons with a third option of no preference?"

"Exactly."

"Easily enough done. We'll have to revisit the panic button thing, but I'll give it some thought."

"Thank you. How's Ffion?"

"So far, I think she's okay. Why? Any updates?"

"Not yet. I'll call you as soon as we have anything. It may take a little time."

"Fair enough. Well, I should probably get to these changes. I'll email you as soon as I have the next version ready. And I mean it, you call me if you start feeling off."

"I will."

I want to trust that she will, but she's the type who could have her arm hanging off with blood spurting from a severed artery and she'd insist it's only a flesh-wound. So, I make a mental note to check in with her tomorrow if she doesn't check in with me first.

EIGHTEEN

Mel

I'm so keyed up after my call with Stuart, I decide to have lunch with Nora, because I could really use some girl talk, and she's the only person on the planet I can chat with about this and trust that it will stay just between us.

We meet at the little deli around the corner from my office.

"What's with the comfort food?" she asks, pointing to my bowl.

"Nothing. I was in a soup mood. Besides, you know I have a weakness for this one."

"Yeah, sure, whatever. Now, really, what's up?"

"I found my app designer."

"Not seeing how that calls for comfort food."

"It's crazy."

She puts down her sandwich and leans back in her seat. "I'm good with crazy. Now spill, bitch."

"He actually turned the project down to start. But then we met up at Silver and—"

"Wait. You set up a meet with this guy at a BDSM club?"

I chuckle. "No. After our meeting, I went there in the hopes of hooking up with a Dom to take me out of my head for a while. Apparently, he had a similar plan. Except he was looking for a sub."

"Are you fucking kidding me? What are the odds?"

"Right? Anyway, he was bloody amazing. And now I don't know what to do. Because smart me says, make with the retreat, post haste. Keep it purely professional, and walk the fuck away. However, kinky me says bring it the fuck on."

"I think you should go with kinky you."

"Not helpful."

"I'm not here to be helpful. My job as your best friend is to enable you. But wait a sec. I thought you said he turned you down."

"He did. But something came up that required my help and in exchange, he agreed to do the app. He had a mock-up of it ready for me when I woke up yesterday. It's amazing. I asked for some changes this morning, but holy shit. It's everything I was hoping for, and so much more."

"And you got yourself a Dom out of the deal."

"Maybe. No. Oh fuck, I'm just so messed up over the entire thing, I don't know which way is up. But I can't wait to see him again even though I know it's the worst possible thing I could do. And I keep finding myself trying to wrangle another trip to Vancouver, just so I can go get my ass all marked up some more."

"So, why fight it? It's been an awfully long time since you've shown any real interest in a man, let alone one who can do the shit you like done to you."

"It's just not professional. I mean, what a cliché!"

"Okay. So, if you hadn't met with him professionally first, if you'd gone to Silver and you two connected there, would you be waffling around like this? Or would you be happily jumping in with both feet?"

"I don't know. I mean, he's obviously a regular at Silver, but I don't recall ever seeing him there. So, does that mean I just didn't notice him? And if so, maybe it's only because I hadn't already met him, and already attracted. Besides, I didn't actually notice him at the club until he approached me."

"You're over-thinking this, you know."

"And you are just a romantic at heart, always on the lookout for the happily ever after."

"And your point? Seriously, what could it hurt to take this thing you've got going with this guy for a ride and see where it leads?"

"What could it hurt? My heart. My reputation. And that's just for starters."

"What's that old saying? She who dares, wins? Come on, I dare you."

"No."

I don't get a chance to say more, because my phone buzzes, and the message is to get my ass back to my office. "Sorry, I've got to go. Duty calls."

"Go save some poor, wretched soul from career suicide. I need to get back to work anyway. Just remember that I'm right here for you if you need to talk. And seriously, maybe try giving this guy a chance. You deserve it."

"Have a great afternoon, and I'll catch you later."

I hurry back to the office to see what disaster needs cleaning up this time.

Wil is leaning back on the small sofa, one ankle resting on the other knee as his finger glides over the surface of his tablet.

"Okay, what's going on?" I ask as I flop down beside him.

"You are not going to believe this. Tara Langston has been dropping hints to the paps that she has a story to tell."

"Well, shit. I knew she was going to be trouble."

"Do you want me to go lean on her?"

"Yeah. She was warned I'd go all scorched earth on her career if she breached the NDA, but maybe she just needs a reminder. If she keeps it up after that, she'll find out just how far my reach is."

"Fair enough. I assume I should keep someone on her for a while longer?"

"Yeah. At least until it's clear she's going to keep her mouth shut or she slinks back to whatever backwater hamlet she crawled out of."

"On it. Anything else?"

"Anything on Ffion's situation?"

"I've got a guy going through her electronics and

someone else catfishing in that chatroom for our asshole. I get it. This one's personal. You'll be the first to know when I've got something solid."

"Thanks."

With a nod he gets up, and as soon as he leaves, I call Eli and order him to continue keeping his ass squeaky clean until I tell him otherwise. Which won't be until Stuart has that app ready for primetime.

NINETEEN

Stuart

I know Mel is good at what she does and I just need to be patient, but it's all I can do to stop myself from constantly bugging her for an update. The first week I had the excuse of a Dom checking in on a sub, and if she happened to volunteer an update, so much the better.

Once her marks were gone, however, it's become a little harder to come up with viable excuses to call.

"It's going to need a name," I tell Mel in my latest phone call.

"Why? It's not like it's going big-time."

"It's still better to be the one in control of what it becomes known as."

"What if I get it wrong?"

"Welcome to the big bad world of apps. I'm going to go out on a limb and suggest that getting it wrong for something that's supposed to be underground isn't as bad as getting it wrong for a product you're looking to make bank on."

"Have you given the name any thought?" she asks.

"Some."

"Okay, what are your ideas?"

"Just one, really. Fetwrk without an O because I find it more aesthetically pleasing. Short for Fetish Network."

"I like it. Let's go with that."

"Will do. How are you doing?"

"Busy, but well. How's Ffion?"

"Still stressed. She's kicking it old-school these days. She calls me from the landline."

"People still have those?"

"Some. Hayden likes to keep it around in case of emergency."

"Huh. Who knew? Hey, I wish I had some good news to share, but these things take time."

TWENTY

Mel

I'm yanked from the most delicious dream by Wil's ring-tone, and I make zero effort to hold back my irritation.

"This had better be good," I growl.

"Is the news that Ffion's internet asshole got picked up by the Mounties for child luring about an hour ago good enough?"

I flip on the light and check the time. Two in the morning. "What damned time zone were they in?"

"Does it matter? Bottom line is, they have this fucker dead to rights. Slam-fucking-dunk. And best of all, there's no chance Ffion should get pulled into it. It's over. He made arrangements to meet up at a motel with our catfisher, who the asshole believed to be an eleven-year-old girl. Using stellar hacking skills, she managed to get into his private messages. So she may have downloaded all of them and anonymously forwarded them on to the local police. And it's entirely possible they were lying in wait for this asshole to show up."

"What if the cops hadn't done anything? Stuart said that they couldn't do anything about this guy regarding Ffion."

"We were prepared for that. But the cops came through in the end."

"Thanks so much, Wil. And thank everyone who worked on this."

"Weird as it sounds, I think everyone liked working on this one. Getting to be the good guys who take a scumbag off the street."

"Yeah, I get it."

"While I've got you here, anything on our friend Ms. Langston?"

"Nope. She's been keeping her head down. Do you want me to stay on her, or...?"

"Maybe just keep tabs on her once in a while for a bit longer?"

"Okay. We done did good, boss lady."

"Yes, we done did."

"I thought about letting you sleep—for about eight seconds. But I knew you'd want to know right away."

"Yeah. Thanks again. I'll see you tomorrow—later this morning. Get some sleep."

I give the thought of letting Stuart sleep the same eight seconds Wil gave me and come to the same decision.

Stuart picks up on the second ring.

"Mel, what's wrong?"

"Sorry, not sorry, but internet asshole was arrested about an hour ago. I just got the call, and I took the chance that you'd prefer to hear about it right away."

"Oh, thank fuck. That's a huge relief. I'll call Hayden right now, but he'll probably wait until Ffion is up to let her know. Thanks Mel. I can't tell you how much this means to us."

"I think I have a pretty good idea. Anyway, glad I could pass along good news. I'll let you go spread it while I go back to dreamland. I'll call you later when I have more details."

"Good night. Sleep well."

TWENTY-ONE

Stuart

The six weeks since Mel and I entered into our agreement have been the longest six fucking weeks of my life, but the app is done, and my contract is complete upon delivery.

Personal delivery.

I'm a little surprised when I enter Mel's office suite. She'd come off so high-powered, I guess I expected something swanky on an upper floor of a tower. Instead, it's on the third floor of a nondescript five-floor building that has zero chance of survival in the event of a reasonably significant earthquake.

The receptionist—Christine Lavelle, according to the nameplate on her desk—looks up and smiles. "Can I help you?"

"Yes, I'm Stuart Cole. I'm here to see Mel."

"Oh, you're the app guy?"

Snobby me tries not to be offended. "Yes."

"Go right on in," she says pointing the door off to my left.

I try not to grin at the shocked look on Mel's face as I walk through the door.

"What are you doing here? How do you know where my office is?"

I just raise an eyebrow and nod down to the box I'm holding.

"App is done, and I've come to set the equipment up for you."

"Doesn't it just get uploaded somewhere like iTunes or Google?"

"Seriously? You ask me to build you a government-grade secure app, availability of which, you want limited, and you think you're going to host it where the entire world can have access?"

"Don't they have VIP tiers and stuff, like dating sites?"

"Mel, please tell me you're joking."

"I am. Sort of?"

"You didn't think about how this was going to roll out beyond installing on smart phones?"

"Not really."

"Then it's a good thing you hired me, because I do think about these things."

I wonder, for just a moment, whether she'd planned this far ahead after all. Based on everything I now know about her, and what she does, she's prepared for plans A through WTF. I let it go. Because it gives me hope that she's onboard for a repeat of our night at Silver.

"How long will it take for you to set all this up?" she asks.

"Five or six hours, if all goes smoothly, why?"

"Because it's Thursday, which means the busiest part of my week will start soon. And since you're here with the goods, I was kind of hoping I could maybe pre-empt some of the crazy by getting as many of my clients hooked up on that app as possible."

"Do they know it's coming?"

"Yeah. I've been feeding details to the right people for a couple of weeks, now."

"Just don't overload the system on the first day." *Or I might have to punish you.*

"I'll be good."

TWENTY-TWO

Mel

"I'm sure you will." Stuart's expression turns almost feral as he stalks toward me. "The project is done. You've saved the day for Ffion. You can't use the excuse of not mixing business and pleasure again, and you can't tell me that one scene together is enough for you."

"No, I can't, on either score. But it's still not a good idea."

"We both did app profiles. Tell me it's possible for there to have been a more compatible couple."

"I can't. But—"

"No more buts. You're just coming up with bullshit excuses because you're scared."

"I'm not scared." Fuck, how can he see through me, so easily?

"You're fucking terrified. You tried to bail in the

middle of me giving you aftercare—one of my favorite parts of a scene, by the way—because you were scared. Try and deny it."

"Fine, so I'm scared. That doesn't mean it's a good idea to try again."

"I think trying again is an excellent idea. Maybe desensitizing you is just what you need."

"Even if I were to agree, there is no club in this city we could ever go to."

"I understand. And it is safer to play in public, for sure. In that case, I want a promise. I need to stay out the week here to deal with any issues that may arise, but I want the first free night you have after that. At Silver. You've played there before, obviously, so no more excuses."

Fuck. I want him so badly, I'd be willing to take a chance on playing in private. But that's exactly how my clients wind up needing my services, and wouldn't that be a helluva thing to have to live down? Not to mention career suicide.

Traveling to Silver? I can do that.

I pull out my phone and check my schedule. "I can swing five days starting a week from this coming Monday through to the Friday morning. It wouldn't hurt for me to meet with clients up there and get them set up with the app."

He pulls me in for a long, hungry kiss which I eagerly return.

"In that case, I want all four of those nights, because I'm a greedy, mean, and evil Dom."

And that right there is exactly why I just cleared most of a fucking week.

TWENTY-THREE

Stuart

When I walk into The Dark Roast just before two on Monday, Mitch has already got our drinks and snagged a table.

"So, what did you want to see me about?" he asks as I sit down.

"Well, I have this idea. What if I built an app to handle limit lists and negotiation for the club? I was thinking we could have dedicated tablets, and the data could be kept on an onsite server. Closed network. Members would have their details readily available, so when negotiating, a potential partner can pull them up. It could also have kind of a quick start guide. Hard limits, compatible loves, that kind of thing."

"On the surface, I like that idea a lot. I'd need to take it to the board, of course, so for that, I'd need a formal proposal."

"I'm happy to put one together, along with a mock-up version."

"Sounds great. Would sure save a lot of time, paper, and pencil sharpening."

"No kidding. It's been a while since we've had a chance to talk. What's new?"

"It's been a while because you haven't been by the club. Life is pretty much same old same old. You, on the other hand..."

"What?"

"You went from swinging by the club at least once a week to being no-show for what must be closing in on two months, now. The last I saw of you was when you were walking out of the club in the company of the very lovely, and very submissive, Mel. So..."

"I'm interested. You might even say, invested, but she's reluctant."

"*Reluctant* is a far cry from the *no way* every other Dom at Silver has experienced when trying to get her to commit to more than the occasional scene."

I have so many questions, but I don't ask because it would be disrespectful to Mel, and potentially, put Mitch in an uncomfortable position.

"There's really nothing new with you?"

He lets out a huge sigh. "I went to my thirtieth high school reunion on the weekend."

"And...?" I rest my elbows on the table and wait for him to continue.

"Oh fuck it. The girl—woman now—I had a real thing for back then was there. Threw me for a loop because it's the first reunion she's attended. Well, there's more to it than that, but I'm still processing."

He looks at his watch. "Shit, I need to get going. If you don't make it to the club, at least don't leave it so long to get together next time."

"Hey, same goes. I don't see anything wrong with your fingers."

Chuckling, he flips me the bird and we both head our separate ways.

I have an app to finish and a proposal to write as well as prepare for Mel's visit.

TWENTY-FOUR

Mel

My belly flutters as I wait for Stuart to pick me up from my hotel. I could have driven myself, but he was insistent that this time, he didn't want to risk me driving because he had plans. And fuck me if I didn't drench my panties at the word *plans*.

The knock on the door takes me a little by surprise. I'd expected him to just text me when he arrived and wait for me in the car.

I slip my coat on over my outfit and open the door. "Hi,"

"Hi. Going to make me wait until we get to the club to see what kind of wrapping my prize is wearing?"

"Yep."

His eyebrow cocks. "What was that?"

"Yes, Sir." He's not going to let me slide on anything, and that just makes me hotter for him. The one regret I had from the last time we played was that we didn't fuck. He didn't even get off.

Unlike me.

"Let's go, then. The sooner we get there, the happier we both will be."

It takes about half an hour to get to the club, and Stuart spends that entire time talking up our night without actually giving me details.

"Restroom, then meet me back here," he says as soon as we're finished checking in.

"I don't need to go, Sir."

"Did you just argue with me?"

"I'm sorry, but—"

"That's five with the cane before we even get started. Would you like to go for more?"

"No, Sir."

"Good. Even though you don't feel the need now, I'll bet once you relax you'll manage just fine. I'm serious when I say I do not appreciate my scenes being interrupted with avoidable bathroom breaks. Understood?"

"Yes, Sir." I hurry off to the restroom, and damn if he wasn't right. Fucker. Five with the cane for arguing is probably better than whatever he'd mete out for interrupting a scene for a bathroom break after refusing one.

"Tonight, I think we'll go with the spanking bench again. I want you fully supported because I'm going to work you over very, very hard."

He pulls a set of cuffs from his bag. They're different from the black ones he used last time. These are a deep, almost burgundy leather with intricate tooling around the edges on the outside and black leather lining inside.

"Special, just for you."

"They're beautiful."

"Just like you. Now, up you get," he says, pointing to the spanking bench.

As soon as I'm settled, he clips my cuffs to the D-rings on the sides.

"We'll go old school to wake up your pink bits while I give you those five cane stripes you owe me," he says as he shows me three wooden clothes pins fanned out in his hands.

I'd almost forgotten about the cane.

The clothes pins are a mild pinch as they go on, but I know from experience they'll pack more punch coming off.

"Color?"

"Green, Sir."

The first cane stroke hits the fleshiest part of my ass and burns like a son of a bitch. I wait and wait for the next one, and just as I think maybe he's changed his mind, and it's not coming, it hits where my ass meets my thighs. The pinch of the clothespins on my nipples and clit regenerates as they jiggle with each stroke, and I'm struggling to process two very different kinds of pain.

The next stroke hits somewhere between the first two. Stuart leans down and gently nips my earlobe. "Such a good girl." The cane gets me again, while my brain is occupied with the new sensation.

By the time Stuart's given me the final stroke, I'm

sure there's nowhere on my ass that's going to want to spend time on a chair.

Meanwhile, the pins have come off my clit, and it burns like fuck.

"You are so beautiful. You have a safeword. Use it if you need to, otherwise you will take everything I give you."

He presses a vibrator against my clit and I do my best to pull away, but his arm is a steel band across my lower back. An orgasm rips through me, and I sob with relief when he pulls the vibe away. My respite is brief, however. As soon as I catch my breath, he's pressing the vibe against my clit again, and I can't control anything. Not my voice, or my body. I'm shaking all over as I scream and cry for him to stop. But he doesn't. He just forces me to come again and again.

"Color?" He asks the next time he pulls the vibe away.

"Green, Sir," I whisper between panting breaths

"Are you sure?"

Am I? "Yes, Sir."

"On we go, then."

As the next orgasm rips through me, he pulls the clothespins off my nipples. The pleasure-pain is off the charts as the blood rushes back into my poor tortured flesh.

This man is a maniac in the best possible way.

By the time he unhooks me, I'm in that lovely floaty place he took me before, and before I know it, I'm snuggled up in his lap.

"Such a good, brave girl. You took everything I gave you so beautifully."

"But you didn't get to come. Again."

"Not every scene needs to end in an orgasm for me. And remember, we're at Silver. There's no ejaculating here."

"Take me home with you?"

"Oh, baby, I want to say yes in the worst way, but you're in no condition to be making decisions like that right now. If we'd negotiated it before playing, I'd have had you out of here quite some time ago. If you feel the same tomorrow, then you can call and ask me for what you want."

I want to argue with him. Convince him I'm perfectly capable of making my own decisions, but his expression tells me in no uncertain terms how big a mistake that would be. His word is final. It doesn't stop me from letting my disappointment show with the poutiest pout I can manage.

"I get it. You're used to getting your own way and you're grumpy I said no. This time, I'll let you get away with the pouts, but only because we haven't discussed the fact that they're no different in my eyes than arguing with me. Also, you're still loopy, and for that I can allow that maybe you're not fully cognizant of what you're doing.

"I know exactly what I'm doing."

"Probably not the best response to give me right now. Especially when you still have plenty of unmarked flesh just yearning for my cane. We have clear rules around punishments, and if you keep that up, loopy or not, you're going to find your ass in a world of hurt."

I shut my mouth, because I have a feeling he's talking about a lot more than five strokes of the cane, and those were hard enough.

TWENTY-FIVE

Stuart

I had a hard time concentrating on work today, knowing what I've got in store for tonight. In the end, I gave up trying and spent the afternoon making sure everything was perfect.

Mel's phone call this morning was not entirely unexpected.

I could practically hear her blushing over the phone, especially when I insisted she be clear about what exactly she wanted.

As soon as I hear her car in the driveway, I go out to meet her and bring in her bag.

We both know exactly why she's here, and her blush is so fucking adorable.

"Why are you embarrassed? You didn't seem uncomfortable at the club."

"I don't know. I just am."

"Okay. Feelings are feelings, and we can't always control them."

As soon as we're inside, I point to the cushion I've placed on the floor just inside the entryway. "Strip and be kneeling on that by the time I get back."

"Yes, Sir."

I hang her coat in the hall closet and take her bag to my bedroom. If I have my way, she's not going to need anything from it besides her toothbrush until she leaves Friday morning. But I'll play that by ear because I have no idea what could come up for her tomorrow.

When I return to the front door, she's folded her clothes and kneeling exactly as she was told. "Very nice. Now, stand please and turn around. I'd like to see what's left of last night."

There are a few faint purple lines across her ass where I'd nailed her particularly hard with the cane. "Any problem sitting today?"

"Only in a good way, Sir."

"Damn. Oh well, the night is young." I chuckle at the slight clench of her butt-cheeks. I don't actually plan on being as hard on her as I was last night. Not just because she took a lot from me, but also because we're not at the club, and I want her to understand that I will only ever play safely with her, regardless of where we are.

"Come with me."

I lead her to the basement, where all good dungeons should live.

While I only play at Silver these days, I did have a sub who lived with me for a long time, and it was more convenient to play at home. Since we split, I've not felt the urge to bring anyone home. Until now.

"Any aches, pains, stiffness I need to know about before we begin?"

"No, Sir."

"Any changes in limits since last night?"

"No, Sir."

"I'm going to step things up a bit tonight." If only because we're going to have sex. "We'll start on the spanking bench, because that's an excellent place to get you all prepped for my pleasure. And it will be my pleasure tonight, little subbie."

"Yes, Sir."

I put her cuffs on but don't bother to clip her to the bench. I stroke my hands all over her back and ass, paying particular attention to my cane marks. I kiss each one. "You were such a good girl for me last night, taking all your cane strokes like a champ."

"Thank you, Sir."

"The club is particular about restricting penetration and ejaculation to privacy rooms to avoid running afoul of any legal authorities, so it's safe to say we'll be concentrating on exactly those things tonight."

Her whole body does a tiny shiver, and her pussy clenches. "Oh, is your pussy feeling empty?"

"Yes, Sir."

"If you're a very good girl, I might do something

about that later. In the meantime, I've been dying to put my plug in that little asshole of yours for months. Tonight, you're going to have to ask me for everything you get. In explicit detail. Is there something you would like?"

"Please Sir, please plug my ass."

"That's not very convincing. Try again."

"Please Sir, please put your plug in my ass."

"It will be my pleasure."

Opening the small drawer in the end of the bench, I grab lube and the plug I selected for her earlier. Everything close at hand where I need it. I have no intention of giving her even the tiniest minute to second-guess herself.

Her sweet little ass clenches as I squirt some lube on her tiny hole.

"We never really discussed your level of anal experience. On a scale where ten is you're an anal slut and the less lube the better, and one is use an entire bottle, and nothing bigger than your pinkie, please, where would you say you are?"

"Eight?"

"Are you sure? Because I will take you at your word, and now is the best time to adjust your rating."

"Eight," she says with more confidence.

"You have no idea how happy that makes me." I squirt a little more lube on her hole and then slather some on the plug. At an eight, she's done this enough that I don't feel the need to finger her up to it. Pressing the tip of the plug against her tiny, puckered entrance, I apply steady pressure, slowly increasing it. When she's stretched almost to the widest point, I push hard, making her squeal.

I never said I was going to make it easy.

"Good girl."

TWENTY-SIX

Mel

If he only knew just how special he makes me feel when he tells me I'm a good girl. Fuck, I'd do and take just about anything for that.

My ass feels really full. Not the biggest plug I've ever taken, but—I cut that thought short. This isn't the time or place to go there.

Stick to the here and now, with Stuart.

"I had a hard time deciding exactly how I wanted this evening to go, but eventually, I figured it out."

I wait for him to continue. To tell me what he has in store. But he says nothing else. I hear him moving behind me, and I resist wiggling my butt.

Some Doms like that kind of thing. He doesn't appear to be that sort. And for that, I'm grateful. I don't want to think. I don't want to top from the bottom. My job demands that I take charge and find creative solutions to the most complicated of problems. When it comes to my sex life, I need someone else to fill that role.

"Tonight, you'll beg me for everything I'm going to do to you. Understood?"

"Yes, Sir."

He holds up a metal dome-shaped apparatus with an open bottom. A clover clamp is suspended in the middle by a threaded bolt that's attached to the top of the dome by a wingnut.

"A lovely variation on the clover clamp theme. The more I tighten the nut, the farther it stretches your nipple while tightening the grip of the clamp on your nipple...or clit. I think we'll just go with nipples today. But you're going to have to beg for it."

"Please torture my nipples with those evil clamps, Sir."

"I don't think you really want it."

"Please, Sir. I really, really want you to do mean things to me with those clamps."

"Good enough."

I let out a long sigh of relief. I don't have a lot of experience at begging and I'm not really liking it. But it's not a limit.

He centers the contraption over my left nipple. I hiss as he attaches the clamp and twists the nut until my nipple is stretched taut.

"Don't hold back on my account. Nothing makes me happier than hearing my sub vocalize her appreciation of my handiwork."

I hiss again when he secures a clamp to my other

nipple, making him chuckle in that deliciously evil way of his.

"Beg me to make them tighter," he demands.

"Please make them tighter, Sir."

"Beg, little subbie."

"Please, I need you to make the clamps tighter."

He gives each nut a full twist visiting fresh hell upon my nipples.

"Lovely," he says as he flicks the cages one by one.

"Oh my. That looks like a wet pussy. Do you want me to fuck you, little subbie?"

"Yes, please, Sir. Please fuck me." I hear the tell-tale crinkle of a condom wrapper.

"Do you want me to pound your little pussy?"

"Please, Sir. Pound my pussy with your cock." Apparently, I have no trouble begging for what I've been wanting from him for months.

"As you wish."

He slams into me with no warning, and while I'm soaking wet for him, I'm not prepared for just how big he is.

He leans over my back and grabs onto my shoulders, using them for leverage as he rams his cock into me over and over and over.

My breasts swing wildly back and forth with each thrust, making my nipples burn.

"Do you want to come, little subbie?"

"Please, Sir. More than anything."

"If you want to come, then you're going to have to

work for it." He reaches between my legs and traps my clit between two fingers.

I try to work my hips in ways to use his fingers, but it's hard while he's slamming his cock into me. And whenever I manage to find a rhythm that's working, he changes his own.

"I don't know that you want it badly enough."

"I do, Sir. I do." I don't bother to keep the whine out of my voice.

"Don't forget to ask permission first."

I work my hips harder and faster and I almost go over before I remember to ask. "Please, may I come, Sir?"

"You may."

His words are just enough to push me over into wave after wave of bliss.

As the final spasms of my orgasm recede, he releases my nipples, letting the cages drop to the floor. His fingers return to my clit, but this time, he doesn't demand I be the architect of my own orgasm.

"One more for me. I want you to come with me this time, little subbie," he whispers in my ear as his hips rock against my ass and his fingers work my clit until we both explode.

TWENTY-SEVEN

Stuart

Fuck. Me.

Mel is everything I could ever ask for in a woman. Her masochism is the perfect complement to my sadism. She's funny, sweet, sexy as hell, and I don't think I could ever get enough of her.

I release her from the bench and carry her to my bedroom. "You've been a very good girl for me, and now it's sleepy time for both of us, little subbie."

She snuggles into me and I hold her close, kissing the top of her head as I try to come up with a way for us to spend more time together.

Except I'm being ridiculously premature. We barely know each other. Kink compatibility is a huge necessity in a relationship, but it's not everything.

The next morning, I wake to an empty bed. Being a

light sleeper, I'm surprised I didn't feel her get up, but I did have a pretty exhausting night.

I pad naked to the living room, where she's sitting on the sofa, talking on the phone. Completely dressed. She holds her finger up and to her lips, and I nod and retreat to the kitchen where I get the coffee started.

It's nearly ready when she joins me.

"You're overdressed. No coffee until you're naked and back in bed."

"Something came up and I have a lunch meeting."

"I'm sure you do, but not before you have coffee, which isn't happening until you're naked and back in my bed. Every second it takes you to get there is a cane stroke."

I count five before she starts removing her clothes. I'm at fifteen by the time she's naked. I continue counting, coffee in hand as I follow her to my room.

"Twenty-seven. I think we'll make it an even thirty. I prefer round numbers."

She opens her mouth to complain, but wisely says nothing.

"Good girl," I say as I pass her one of the mugs. "And because I'm feeling benevolent, I'll postpone your caning until tonight."

"Thank you, Sir."

"You're welcome. Now come here." Holding my arm up, I make space for her to snuggle into my side before I start telling her all the dirty, kinky, evil things I want to do to her and with her.

TWENTY-EIGHT

Mel

My meeting turns out to be mercifully short. Stuart meets me at the door and pulls me in for a long, very thorough kiss before dragging me into the house. My belly flutters and I push down all the feelings I have.

"What did you bring?" he asks as he takes the box from me.

"Only the best cookies in the world."

We're sitting at the kitchen table and he's pouring tea into my mug when he asks the question I knew would come, but kind of hoped it wouldn't.

"So, what made you want to become a fixer? Because that's probably not even in the top hundred answers kids give when asked what they want to be when they grow up."

I consider giving him my stock answer—that I just kind of fell into it. That my law practice just kind of slid in that direction. But something makes me decide to tell him the whole truth instead of the sanitized, truncated version of it.

"My best friend's parents and my parents were very close friends. Our families spent a lot of time together. Lots of parties. Some at our house, but most at theirs. Nora and I would sneak onto the mezzanine and watch, even though we were supposed to be sleeping. Sometimes, the parties were in the big rec-room in Nora's basement. We never got to watch any of those parties because there was nowhere for us to hide. One night—we were about Ffion's age—it was out in the backyard by the pool, and well, we both got one hell of an education. There was a full-on orgy going on down there.

"Later that night, my mother came barreling into Nora's room, packed us both up, and spirited us away to our house. Turned out Nora's bad feeling had been bang-on. A paparazzo had found himself a perch from which to take photos. My parents' kick-ass lawyer fixed it so those photos never saw the light of day.

"Anyway, it was the lawyer who made me want to help others from being ruined for doing things that aren't morally or legally wrong. So, while I usually tell people that I kind of slid into the role over time, the reality is I steered my practice very carefully. I may be one of the very few kids on the planet who wanted to be a fixer when I grew up, but I did realize I needed to be a lawyer first."

"You're still close with Nora?"

"Yeah. She's been my best friend for as long as I can

remember. I'm one month older. I wasn't kidding when I said our families did everything together. We still get together as much as we can. But she keeps her head down and her nose clean. I try to protect her in my own way, and now we've got this app, I'll get her set up with it."

"But I thought she's keeping her head down and avoiding Hollywood."

I grin at him. "I want the option to be there for her. She needs someone in her life other than her cat and her vibrator."

"You're a good person, Mel Seymour."

"I try."

"Thank you for telling me the real story instead of the press-release version."

"I trust you. And I wanted you to know what makes me tick. Give you a little peek through the window to my soul."

Stuart nods and opens his mouth to say something, but his phone starts ringing.

"It's Ffion. I need to take this."

"Of course you do." As I start to get up to leave and give him some privacy, he tugs me back down as he answers. I pull out my own phone and check email until he's done.

"Ffion wants to go to the beach. And she'd like you to come too."

"I'm a California girl. It's way too cold for the beach."

"For lounging around on a towel wearing a bikini, sure. But we're going hunting for sea-glass, pretty pebbles, and other interesting things that may have washed up on shore. I'll even sweeten the pot and postpone your caning until tomorrow night."

We spend a lovely couple of hours just wandering along the beach, stopping every so often when something interesting catches our eye and sifting through pebbles.

After we drop Ffion at home, we swing by the local grocery store.

"You're so good with her. Why no kids?" I ask.

"I have her, and she's...everything. Besides, even if I did want kids, which I don't, I've been short on a critical component to the kid making process. So, I'm perfectly happy to have one I can spoil rotten and send home after. What about you? Why no kids?"

"I don't lead the kind of life that would be good for kids to grow up in. My job would mean I'd either have to have a full-time nanny, or a partner who could hold down the fort on zero notice. And there's no way I'd want that for my kids or my partner."

TWENTY-NINE

Mel

"You look exhausted." Stuart ushers me into his house the next afternoon.

"I am. With some people, it's an uphill battle."

"Come sit down."

When I sit next to him on the sofa, he pulls my feet into his lap and digs his thumbs deep into the soles, working out every knot.

"Oh my god, I could just lie here and let you do this for the rest of my life."

"Careful what you wish for."

"I can't imagine wishing for a lifetime of foot massages could be a bad thing."

"From a sadist, you never really know, do you?"

Hello, masochist here. "Fair point. How was your day?"

"It was fine. Would have been finer with you in it, but I'm a selfish fuck and just want you all to myself."

"Pretty sure my day would have been a damn sight better if I'd spent it here with you."

"I have you for the rest of the afternoon and all night, though, right, little subbie?"

Two little words and he can totally flip my switch. "Yes, Sir."

He unfastens his jeans and frees his erection. "I've been waiting all day to see how well you suck cock. I think it's time I found out, don't you?"

I lick my lips. "Yes, Sir."

"No teeth, or I'll fit you with an O-ring gag."

I hate gags with a passion. They're not a hard limit, but I go out of my way to make sure I don't wind up wearing one.

He's a sadistic Dom, and I expect he'll take charge soon enough, so, I'm going to get all the jollies I can before he does.

I swirl the tip of my tongue around the crown, flick it over his slit, and then bob up and down, before teasing him with my tongue again.

"That's lovely, little subbie, but I've been waiting for this all day and my patience is beginning to wear thin. Unless you want me to take over, you'd best make me come in the next two minutes."

I slide up and down his cock, taking him deep. I have decent deep throat skills, but it never hurts to keep a little something in reserve, and if I can make him blow within my time limit without? Then, go me.

As I move faster and suck harder, I feel his cock swell a bit. "Take it all, little subbie. I want you to swallow everything I give you."

Holding the back of my head, he stops me from pulling back as he thrusts his hips upward, holding his cock in my mouth until I swallow the last spurt of come.

"Good girl. You did well."

"Thank you, Sir."

"Strip. No clothes until you leave tomorrow."

Once I'm naked, he pulls me into his lap and kisses me.

"You've been a good girl this afternoon, but you have transgressions to pay for from yesterday morning. What is your punishment and why?"

"I hesitated when you gave me an order, and that earned me a cane stroke for every second it took me to get naked and back into your bed. It took me twenty-seven seconds, which you very *generously* rounded up to thirty."

"Very good, even if you are a bit cheeky. Are you ready to take your punishment now?"

"Yes, Sir."

"Ask me for it."

"Please may I have the thirty cane strokes I earned yesterday morning, Sir?"

"With pleasure. Come with me."

Eagerly, I follow him down to the dungeon.

"Stand there, feet shoulder-width apart and offer me your breasts, little subbie"

I cup the underside of my breasts and hold them up.

"Your breasts will take ten of your strokes. Five each. You may scream and cry and make all the noise you need to, but you will stand perfectly still. Understood?"

"Yes, Sir."

By the time a flash of pain registers on my right breast, he's laid a stripe on my left. And on it goes—the pain from one breast registers as he strikes the other, confusing the fuck out of my brain. Meanwhile, my voice is the only reaction I'm allowed, so that's where I focus all my pain.

"Such a good girl, little subbie. I know that was hard for you. The next fifteen will be across your ass and thighs. Fortunately, I left plenty of space to add more of my marks to your beautiful skin. Bend over, legs spread wide enough for you to put your palms on the floor and hold yourself steady."

Once I'm in position, he pushes me gently this way and that to ensure I'm well balanced.

"Again, you may not move, but you may make as much noise as you need. However, this time, you must count your strokes. If you lose count, or take too long to count, we will go back to the beginning."

"Yes, Sir."

His rhythm is similar to how he caned my breasts, so as each stroke lands, I feel the pain of the previous one. Again, I scream, but I'm aware that if I take too long, we'll start the count again, and the closer we get to fifteen, the less I scream.

"Fifteen, Sir," I cry as I work to catch my breath.

"Such a good girl. I'm proud of you for taking your

punishment like a champ. I'd have been prouder if you hadn't earned it in the first place, because it has interfered with my plans. But, I'm nothing if not flexible. Which is why I'm going to cheat slightly with the last five. On your back, pull your knees wide and toward your chest."

I drop to the floor quickly and do as he says.

"Five on your clit with the evil stick. You should know the drill by now, all the noise you want, but you remain absolutely still."

"Yes, Sir."

"And you will count. It's only to five, so I don't expect you to have any difficulties."

"Yes, Sir."

Kneeling between my legs, he's holding a long, black stick, maybe a foot or so long, and thinner than a chopstick. He pulls back one end and when he lets go, my clit explodes with a pain I can't quite process.

"I didn't hear you count. Do we need to start again, little subbie?"

"I'm sorry. One, Sir."

Before I can completely catch my breath, he releases the end of the evil stick again I get an instant rush making my head feel light, almost empty.

"How can you lose count already?"

"Two, Sir. Two, Sir. Two, Sir."

"Make me wait again, and we go back to one, Sir. Understood?"

"Yes, Sir."

He nails me again, and I manage to squeak out,

"Three, Sir," before he has a chance to remind me. Two more. Just two more. I can do this. I may never want anyone or anything to come in contact with my clit ever again, but I can do this.

By the time we get to five, I'm almost hyperventilating. "Good girl. I know that was particularly hard. I hope you learned your lesson."

"Yes, Sir. It's always better to obey you immediately. Thank you for your most thorough instruction."

"You're welcome, little subbie," he says as he scoops me into his arms and carries me off to his bedroom.

Laying me carefully on the bed, he slides in beside me and kisses his way along my shoulder and up my neck before cupping my chin and giving me the sweetest, gentle kiss.

He palms my breast and tweaks my nipple between his fingers before sliding his hand down my belly and sliding a finger between my slick folds. "Are you wet for me, Mel?"

"Yes, Sir."

"No more 'Sir' tonight."

"Yes, I'm wet for you."

He delves deeper until his finger dips inside. He slides it out and circles my clit before slipping it back in. Over and over, almost lazily. As he presses his finger into me, I lift my hips to take him deeper. I expect admonishment. Instead, he adds a second finger without losing a beat. He kisses his way down to my breasts and gently sucks on my nipples one after the other.

"I need to be inside you." He reaches for a condom

from the nightstand, and then hands it to me and he rolls onto his back. "Put it on and ride me."

As soon as I roll the condom down his shaft, I position myself over him and slide down until he's all the way in. Taking hold of my breasts, he squeezes them and pinches my nipples while I slide up and down his cock, making sure to grind my clit against him every time I bottom out.

He nips at my skin wherever he can reach. "Harder and faster. Take everything you want."

His words are the catalyst for the orgasm that starts building low in my belly. I move faster and grind harder until I'm hurtling towards bliss. It hits me so hard, my rhythm skips and I can't hold back the low, gravelly moan, but by this point, Stuart is pumping his hips up into me. His grip on my breasts tightens as he keeps my orgasm going long after I'd have thought it was done. I collapse, panting onto Stuart's chest and he grabs my caned ass hard, making me screech as he fucks up into me. "One more. Give me one more," he growls in my ear. My second orgasm comes almost out of nowhere and Stuart's follows hard on its heels.

We lay there for a few minutes. Breathing hard and heavy. Spent. I'm just edging off to sleep when Stuart rolls us over onto our sides. "Sleep baby. I'm just going to take care of this condom and I'll join you.

I wake up just a bit as Stuart slides in under the covers. He settles his arm over me, and cups a breast as he pulls me back against his chest.

THIRTY

Stuart

It's Friday morning, and our time is up. She has to be back in LA by early afternoon, and chaining her up in my dungeon was, sadly, not an option.

So, here we are at the airport, saying goodbye. Again.

"I had a really good time," she says against my chest.

"Me too. I'm glad you came. And came, and came."

She giggles and I know she's bright red somewhere in my shirt.

"Seriously, I'd really like to get together again. Whatever works for you. You're always welcome to stay with me here, or if you're comfortable playing at your place, I can stay in a hotel and show up as needed."

"Let me think on it. Okay? Everything about LA is more complicated. I'm more accessible to clients there."

"Take all the time you need. I'm in no rush."

"Okay." There's an announcement and we look at each other. "That's my flight."

"Yeah. Safe journey. Text me when you get home, little subbie."

"Yes, Sir."

I give her one last kiss before she pulls away and gets into the line for security.

I watch as she shuffles forward with the rest of the crowd, and we wave one last time before she disappears through the doorway.

My house feels empty and wrong when I get home. Too full of amazing memories, so I call Ethan and meet him for coffee at the Starbucks around the corner.

"What's up, Stu?"

"Did you ever meet someone who's absolutely perfect for you, but the universe sees fit to make that person unattainable?"

"Yep. Until I moved heaven and fucking earth to foil the universe."

"Kelly?"

"Hell yes, Kelly. We lived in different cities. She was pretty leery of my relationship with Heather and Joel. She didn't want to get in the way of our threesomes, if you can believe it. She didn't want to be the poly equivalent of a home-wrecker."

"How did you get past it?"

"With lots of hard work and commitment. On both sides. Mel?"

"Yes, Mel. Hollywood versus Hollywood North."

"You've not been seeing each other long though, have

you?"

"A few months." If I count from the first time we played. Which I do. "But when you know, you know."

"True that. I was hooked on Kelly the first time I met her. She was on a date with some asshole. I was on a date with Heather and Joel at the same place."

"Seriously?" I'd never actually heard the story of how they hooked up before.

"Yeah. To be fair, she was done with the guy before we actually met. It was their second date, and he'd been a complete shithead. Heather intervened because we were all concerned for her. Anyway, sometime down the road, I fucked up and nearly lost her for good. I was too chickenshit to jump in with both feet and commit to her fully, and the universe used that to teach me a hard, hard lesson. Learn from my mistake, my friend. Take a good hard look at how you feel about her. Then ask yourself what you're willing to sacrifice to be with her. If the answer is less than everything, then she's not for you."

Fuck.

"I've had her to myself for the better part of the last three days and nights. I just dropped her off at the airport and I can't stand to be in my house. It just feels wrong. Missing something. Someone. Her."

"Can you go to her for a while?"

"I can, but it will significantly affect how much work I can do. Most of it has to be done in my office at home."

"I get it. Ultimately this is something you're going to have to work out for yourself, but I'm always here anytime you need to talk. Cuz I have been there."

THIRTY-ONE

Mel

I've been melancholy since I kissed Stuart goodbye in the airport. It could be sub-drop, but probably more like Stuart-drop.

It's ridiculous how attached to him I've become in such a short time. I guess when you know, you know.

But having bailed so many people out of sketchy situations, I'm leery of my feelings.

When I get home, I try to throw myself into work. And fail. I open the freezer and eye up the carton of ice cream before heading over to Nora's.

One look at my face as she opens the door, and she yanks me inside. "Go sit down. I'll be back with wine. This clearly looks like a job for day-drinking."

She returns a few minutes later with a bottle of red and two glasses. "Spill," she says as she hands me a very full glass.

"I don't know. I just got back from spending part of the week at Stuart's and I just don't know."

"What is it you think you need to know?"

"If I knew that…"

"Yet again, you're overthinking this. How does he make you feel?"

"Scared."

"How so?"

"I have these feelings. New and unfamiliar feelings."

Nora chuckles and I give her a sour look. "What's so funny about that?"

"Sweetie, for probably the first time ever, you're not completely in control and seeing you so discombobulated, for me, is awesome and yes, funny."

"It is a bit funny, isn't it?"

"Mel, it's time you let someone in. You've always been so very careful with your feelings. I get that your job makes you far more wary than you otherwise might have been over the years, but maybe now you can take these newfound feelings out for a spin?"

"Okay—enough. If I wanted to talk about my feelings, I'd go see a therapist. What about you? Have you been using that app?"

Her blush is adorable.

"Maybe."

"Did you meet anyone worth hooking up more than once?"

"I did."

"Jesus, what's with the one- and two-word answers? This is me. We've always told each other everything."

"And yet, you changed the subject when it comes to whatever it is you have going on with app-guy."

"Busted. Come on, though. Give me something to take my mind off missing him already."

"Well first of all, the app is brilliant. Once I got over my fear of getting caught out, I've actually hooked up with a few guys."

"And more than once with at least one."

"Well, it's just sex. Seriously good sex, but that's all it is."

"Sounds like it's perfectly uncomplicated." Unlike what I'm feeling for Stuart.

"Just the way I like it. Now, if we're done not talking about how we feel about the men in our lives, we've got some serious drinking to do.

THIRTY-TWO

Mel

Sometimes, like today, I wish I could just say fuck it and barricade myself in with Stuart. My house, his house, I wouldn't care.

Sometimes, like today, I wish I could ignore the ringing of my phone.

I'm barely twelve hours in on the four days I was supposed to have with Stuart.

I look at the caller ID and manage to keep the irritation out of my voice when I answer. "Seymour."

"Mel, Janet Gilroy. I need you to go to London. Lis is in a bit of bother—compromising photographs."

"How the hell did that happen? She's got the app."

"Well, I haven't given it to her yet."

"Why the fuck not?"

"Well, she was already on location overseas when the app went live, and I thought—"

"You thought wrong. I'm going to put you in touch with Winston Frobisher, and he'll take care of everything."

"No. I need it to be you. I don't care how much it costs. You're the only one I can trust to make this go away."

There's clearly no point telling her that Frobisher will end up being the one who actually cleans up this mess. She's determined. "Fine. But I'm charging you double plus my expenses."

"Thank you. I'll let Lis know to expect you, and I'll text you her contact information."

"I'll be in touch."

Two hours later, after Stuart gives me a long, lingering kiss goodbye in the airport, I breeze through security and settle my ass in the first-class lounge to wait for my flight to board.

My flight is pleasant enough, and I even manage to grab a decent nap, so I'm not feeling like a complete bag of shit when I arrive on the other side of the Atlantic.

Normally my trips to London involve a visit to Limits, an exclusive BDSM club I hold a membership to. But this thing I have going on with Stuart has me reluctant to go. It would feel too much like cheating, even if I only go to socialize. We talked about it, and he told me he trusts me. But still...it doesn't feel right, and I'm a believer in if it doesn't feel right, don't do it.

If only more of my clients lived by that philosophy, maybe I'd still be in Vancouver with Stuart instead of on the other side of the world cleaning up another unfortunate mess.

Notifications of every kind flood my phone the moment I take it off airplane mode. I check texts first, as I can do that easily enough while I wait to deplane.

Most are from Janet, each one more impatient than the last. Honestly, some people seem to have zero comprehension of time zones and how much longer it takes to fly from the west coast than the east.

Winston Frobisher works from his home, and I still can't get used to being greeted at the door by a butler.

I suppose it's not much different from a receptionist in an office, except I have a feeling I'd seriously offend the guy if I were to actually say that to his face.

"If you'll come this way, Mr. Frobisher is waiting for you in his study." The way the butler says 'is waiting' makes it sound as if I'm an hour late, rather than ten minutes early. I try to shrug it off, but it does rankle.

"Mel, lovely to see you. It's been far too long. Would you like coffee?"

"Coffee would be great, thanks."

"Nigel, two coffees, and some nibbles, if you please."

"Yes, sir."

"Do sit down, Mel." Winston offers me a seat on the leather sofa as he comes out from behind his desk to join me. "So, what is it we're dealing with?"

"Compromising photos and classic blackmail. I've

brought you everything she had." I hand over an enve-lope. "I've convinced Lis you're every bit as good at this job as I am, and it's ridiculous and unnecessary for me to act as a go-between."

Winston nods and has a quick look at the contents of the envelope.

"I'll get someone working on this right away. Now, I understand you have something interesting to show me."

"Indeed, I do." I grin at him because I know he's going to be ecstatic.

"It's a special phone app for public figures with off-brand sexual proclivities to hook up with little risk of finding their secrets plastered over the front pages of the tabloids and gossip sites."

His face lights up, just as I expected it would.

"And when will this be available?"

"It's been up and running for some time in the US, and so far, it's working very well."

"And how are users introduced?"

"I contact agents and managers I've worked with, much like I'm doing with you right now, and set them up with access to the portal so they can install it for their clients as they see fit."

"I see," he says just as the door opens and the butler enters carrying a tray of coffee and scones which he sets on the coffee table.

"Thank you, Nigel, I think that will be all for now."

"Very good, sir."

Picking the mug closest to me, I take a long sip. For a Brit, he serves a pretty decent cup of Joe.

"Scone?" Winston asks, holding out the plate laden with baked mounds of heaven.

I take one and split it before laying the two halves on a plate and loading them with clotted cream and jam. There are some things you just don't count calories for, and a decent scone with all the trimmings is one of them.

"It is serendipitous that you happen to be in London. Lady Charlotte Grey has got herself into a spot of trouble, and in this case, she would be better served by you than me."

"I understand."

He leads me up the stairs and down a long hall. We stop at the last door on the right, and he knocks. "Lady Charlotte, I have Mel Seymour here. May she come in?"

"Yes, please," comes the quiet, shaky reply from behind the thick wood.

I open up, and my heart cracks at the sight.

"Okay, sweetie, let's get this sorted out."

THIRTY-THREE

Mel

Early the next afternoon, I'm on my flight back to Vancouver as originally planned. The Lady Charlotte thing last night was a case of the poor thing just not being comfortable articulating the entire issue to a man. Not even one as sweet and understanding as Winston. Really, all she'd needed was a conduit and I left the matter in Winston's capable hands. That said, there were aspects of the situation that Winston and I agreed were disturbingly similar to Lis's problem.

Stuart is waiting for me when I clear customs with my luggage, and it makes me feel all mushy inside. "Hey," I say as I approach him.

"Hello you." He pulls me in for a smoldering kiss and then whispers in my ear. "I'm going to do very bad things to you after we get home."

"I can't wait."

"Wake up, sleepyhead. We're home." I'm momentarily disoriented before I realize we're in Stuart's car, outside his house.

"I'm sorry, I fell asleep."

"I'm not surprised. Come on, let's get inside." I follow Stuart into the house, and as soon as he shuts the front door behind us, he points down the hall. "Bedroom, now. I want you naked and in my bed."

I don't waste any time obeying his order, because I missed him, even though I was only gone for a couple of days.

He frowns slightly when he walks in. "I told you to get in bed, not on the bed." His voice is stern, but it's laced with love.

"I'm sorry, Sir."

"Just get into bed. There's nothing I want more right now than to bury myself deep inside your body and make you come for days. But you're exhausted, and when I take you, I want you to be fully awake and present."

"But you said you were going to do very bad things when we got home."

"I said *after*, and I didn't say how long after. So, little subbie, the sooner we go to sleep, the sooner I can have my evil way with you."

"Yes, Sir."

The thing about jet lag is that it's unpredictable. Which is why I find myself wide awake at four in the morning and at loose ends.

I shimmy down the bed until my face is level with his

cock. He's sleeping with a semi as it is, so why not take it all the way?

Wrapping my fingers around his growing erection, I take the head into my mouth and suck gently. His hands find the back of my head and press as his hips flex upward.

"Not exactly what I had in mind for this time of the morning, but I can be flexible. Take me deep, little subbie. You want my cock in your mouth, you'll take it all."

I swallow against the gag and heave as he pushes his cock into my throat. I love it when he forces me to take it. I don't understand why, and sometimes it's best not to try and analyze.

He pumps in and out of my mouth, gradually picking up speed. "That's it, sweetheart, I'm nearly there."

A few thrusts later, he holds my face tight to his belly as he empties his balls down my throat.

"Such a good girl. Now, since you're so wide awake, how about you go make the coffee. By the time we're done, I'll be ready to do all the bad things I've been planning since you left."

"Yes, Sir."

Stuart is dozing when I return with our coffee and I'm reluctant to wake him. His eyes pop open at the sound of me putting the mugs on the bedside table.

"Such a good, good girl. I missed you terribly while you were gone. Next time, maybe I should travel with you."

I consider this for a moment. If he'd been with me, we

could have gone to play at Limits. "Yes, maybe you should." I snuggle up to him and he wraps his arm around my shoulders and pulls me in tight.

We drink our coffee in comfortable silence, cuddled up together. I like that we don't feel the need to fill dead air with meaningless conversation.

A little while later, Stuart drains his mug and puts it on his nightstand. "Right, little subbie, drink up. I've got big plans, and I'm ready to get started."

I swallow the last of my coffee, and as soon as the mug is safely on my nightstand, Stuart pounces.

THIRTY-FOUR

Stuart

I don't know why Mel being away in the UK for two days was worse for me than her being down in L.A. for weeks at a time. But it was. And I spent those two days feeling like I need to reclaim my territory. Reassert my dominance over her.

Make it absolutely clear that she is mine.

The wakeup call this morning was a very nice surprise, and I think I may make it a rule that she blows me every time she's not sleeping at some ungodly hour, no matter the reason.

"On your knees, ass up high, little subbie," I demand as I liberate my belt from my jeans. "For your sake, and mine, I should have sent you off with a long-lasting reminder of who you belong to. I won't make that mistake again. These are going to be hard and fast. No need to count, because I won't be stopping until I'm ready to stop or you tap out. Tell me your safeword."

"Red to stop, yellow to check in."

"Good enough. They're going to hurt, so make as much noise as you need. Here we go."

Doubling up the belt, I pull my arm back and let loose a full swing, making her yelp, which in turn makes my cock throb.

The next swing lands just below the first, and the one after that, above. I continue in that fashion until all the flesh of her ass is good and red. I'm tempted to rearrange her over the end of the bed so I can do the same to her thighs, but then decide I'd rather have them available to work over tomorrow when her ass will be too tender to go full bore.

Instead, I start at the beginning and do her ass all over again, all the delicious sounds of her cries and yelps and groans. Her ass is a lovely shade of scarlet by the time I've gone a full second round, but I'm still not satisfied, so I cover her flesh in welts one last time.

"So beautiful. How are you doing, little subbie?"

"Green, Sir."

"Floaty at all?" I ask as I rub my hands all over her angry flesh, savoring the heat radiating off her skin.

"Getting there."

Reaching into my nightstand drawer, I pull out a condom and the bottle of lube. I roll the condom on, then slather my dick with lube. I slide my slick fingers up and down in the crease of her ass before pressing the tip of my cock against her tiny entrance.

"I'm not going to be gentle with you, little subbie. I'm going to make sure you're mine in every fucking way. I want you to feel it for days to come. Are you good with that?"

"Yes, please, Sir."

Leaning in, I exert steady pressure against the tight ring of muscle. "Do not keep me out, little subbie." Eventually she starts to relax, and I press harder.

When the head finally pops in, I slam home, and she lets out a long, loud high-pitched "No!"

I stop, holding myself deep in her ass. "Is that a safeword, Mel?"

"No, Sir," she manages after a few panting breaths.

"Do you need to safeword?" I ask, to clarify.

"No, Sir."

"Then take what I give you."

"Yes, Sir."

I pull back and thrust hard. With one hand on her shoulder, the other on her hip for leverage, I pump into her, hard and deep and without mercy until I can no longer hold back my orgasm. As soon as I'm done, and can catch my breath, I pull out gently and take off to the bathroom. Once I've ditched the condom, I take a warm, wet cloth to Mel, and clean her up.

"How are you doing, little subbie?"

"Great, Sir."

"Even with a sore ass?"

"Even with, Sir."

"I guess you might like it if I let you come once or twice, huh?

"Yes please, Sir."

THIRTY-FIVE

Mel

Stuart and I are recuperating from a late night with a lazy afternoon snuggle when my phone goes off.

"I'm sorry, I need to check that."

"Do what you need to."

"Seymour."

"Mel, turn on the TV," Wil practically yells down the phone.

"What's going on?" I ask as I scramble for the TV remote, hit the power button and switch it to the twenty-four-hour entertainment news channel.

"Oh. My. God."

"Yeah, thought you hadn't already seen that. It's everywhere, and not all the versions are being censored, but conveniently, no identifiable footage of the guy."

Of course not, but I'd bet my last nickel it's Felix

Alexander, scumbag Hollywood power-elite. "Thanks for the heads up." I disconnect and toss the phone on the bed.

"Jesus Mel, are they playing porn on there now?" Stuart asks, his eyebrows pretty much mingling with his hairline.

"It appears someone made a sex tape with Calliope Muir and has released it everywhere. Some places are airing it without leaving anything to the imagination—except who the guy is."

"So, I guess you need to jump on a plane and go get her out of trouble, then?"

"Not until I'm called in."

"But—"

"That was just one of my staff making sure I was aware of the situation."

"So you can get ahead of it?"

"Not exactly. I don't do anything until I'm hired for the job. I do, however, like to know what I might be in for before I get the call."

"I can't imagine what that poor woman is going through right now."

"All I can say is—fuck. What is she doing? No. No. No. Shut up. Shut up and walk away, right now."

And right there, with one extremely ill-advised ad hoc press statement, she strips away any doubt I may have had that it was Felix, and just put herself at more risk.

"Mel, you're going to stroke out if you're not careful."

"God deliver me from actors who think they can handle their own god damn PR." And for the love of the little gold statue, somebody fucking call me to fix this before it becomes completely irreparable.

THIRTY-SIX

I love that Mel is so passionate about making things better for people, but in the days since Calliope Muir's video hit, she has been getting progressively crankier.

"I just don't get it. In all the years I've known Janet Gilroy, this is the first time she's failed to bring me in to fix the shit her clients got themselves into." Mel paces the kitchen floor like a caged tiger.

"You could call and ask her," I finally suggest. Up until now, I'd kept my mouth shut and just let her vent. But it's come to a point where it's doing nothing beyond amping up her emotions.

"I could. But this is Hollywood. There's no way I'd get a straight answer. Besides, she's no longer Calliope's agent. This is such a fucking mess."

"Then you really only have two options. Step in unsolicited or walk away."

"Not helpful."

"Neither is pacing the length and breadth of the house grumbling about the inaction of others."

"I don't need this from you."

"Actually, you do. You have no room in your life for a yes man. It would drive you bonkers if I just sat here patting you on the shoulder and saying 'there, there'. You're actually wandering around like you're the one who's been wronged. It's not about you, Mel."

"I know."

"Yet, you're complaining about how you haven't been contacted to fix a problem."

She stops pacing and stares at me, then shakes her head.

"Come here," Snagging her hand, I her tug into my lap and cradle her head against my chest. "You are a good person with a very kind heart. You're also a very savvy business owner. A combination that doesn't always mix smoothly. I know this is stressing you out, but you need to figure out a way to handle this that works best for you."

Nodding, she wraps her arms around me. "You were right, you know."

"About what?"

"I'd totally hate you being a yes man."

THIRTY-SEVEN

I call in Wil Johnston. I want him to get a jump-start on the situation so I'm not playing catch-up when the call finally comes in.

"What's up?" he asks as he walks into my office.

"The Calliope Muir thing. It's time to get a handle on it."

"Did someone finally call you in? Did she get a new agent."

"No."

"Mel, it's been over a week since it went public, If someone were going to bring you in in this, they'd have done it by now."

"Still..."

"Mel, how many times have you said you can only fix the shit people want fixed?"

"I know. But now I've got this awful feeling that she's

been betrayed by the one person whose sole purpose is to protect the careers of her clients. A purpose for which she is very well paid."

"If you're not called in, then you don't get paid. You know as well as I do, if you do one pro-bono job, you're going to wind up doing more."

"Damn you, Wil. You're right, but Jesus, I feel so guilty for not stepping in."

"I'd lose a lot of respect for you if you didn't."

"I'll stay out of it. But maybe we should be keeping tabs on Felix Alexander. His reprehensible behavior has been one of those open secrets for a lot of years, and there will be a point where someone is finally going to go public, and it would be nice to be able to help when the time comes."

"That sounds like an excellent idea to me. A much better use of pro bono work. I hate what he did to Calliope, I really do. But I don't think there's much we can do to help her now, anyway. That horse bolted from the stable at a gallop and there's no reining it in now."

"Right then, you get someone thoroughly discreet and incorruptible digging into Felix. I know you've worked hard to ensure you have the best of the best on your team, but even so, for the right price, some are more susceptible to bribery than others, and if Felix gets so much as a whiff that we're looking into him, he's going to pull out all the stops to turn your guy."

"I know just the person. It'll be fine."

"Keep me updated as you go along."

"Will do. Anything else?"

"Not right now."

"Then I'll get started on this."

"You're sure it's the right thing to leave Calliope swinging in the wind like this?"

"You have a good heart, Mel. But, at this point, I think it's too late to salvage much of her career, and it could damage your reputation. She's still young and she's not shown herself to maintain a particularly lavish life-style, so she'll be fine."

"Okay. Just get the goods on that motherfucker."

"I'll do my best."

"That's all I can ask."

THIRTY-EIGHT

Stuart

I spend almost every waking hour for the next three weeks buried in a project for the Canadian government. I have five weeks to complete it, but if I can get it done in the next six days, I can steal a week in L.A. with Mel.

I miss her like crazy. Even though she'd only been here full-time for a week, it surprises me how often I catch myself wanting to tell her something. Sometimes I text her, but it's not the same. If I texted her everything I want to say, she'd probably block me for constantly bombarding her.

So I censor myself. Most of the time I write the text, second- and third-guess myself, and delete it.

I want to spend more time with her. Real time. Not honeymoon time. I want to be around when she gets home from work. I want to be there to soothe her when she's had a bad day. I want to keep her adorable little ass covered in my marks.

THIRTY-NINE

Mel

I'm surprised and thrilled to see Stuart when I open the door.

"Why didn't you tell me you were coming?"

"Because I wanted to see your face, to know for sure whether you'd be happy to see me."

"And am I?"

"If you're not, you deserve an Oscar."

"I am very happy to see you. But if I'd known you were coming, I'd have cleared my schedule."

"I don't want you to clear your schedule. I want things to be real with us. And part of that is fitting us into all the other parts of our lives, not stuffing them in a closet so they don't get in the way"

"Come inside. The front step is not the place to have this conversation."

I gesture for him to come inside.

"Do I get you to myself tonight?"

"Entirely."

"Good. Because this last week without you has been hell, and I want to take my time with you. Strip."

As soon as I'm naked, he tangles his fingers in my hair, and pushes me to my knees.

"I've missed your sweet mouth, little subbie."

I deftly unfasten his jeans and pull out his erection.

"Open, I'm driving." His hand pushes my head forward until his cock is touching the back of my throat. "All the way, this time, little subbie. I won't accept anything less." Holding my head still, he presses forward with his hips, forcing his cock down. I relax my throat, swallowing against him as he presses deep.

"That's right, little subbie. Always such a good girl for me."

He pulls his hips back, then pushes forward, harder and faster than before. I continue to swallow against him, loving the groan he makes as I do.

"I'm not going to last. I've gone too long without you."

His hips speed up and I work to keep up with him. "Take everything I give you." He holds his groin tight against my face and I keep swallowing as he empties himself deep in my throat.

When he pulls out, he sinks to his knees in front of me.

"I've missed you so much, little subbie. So much."

"I've missed you, too."

"Even when I cane your tits?

"Yes, Sir."

"Even when I force you to come until you beg me to stop?"

"Yes, Sir."

"What about when I take the evil stick to your clit?"

"Even then, Sir."

FORTY

Stuart

After that amazing blowjob, we relax on the sofa and I give Mel a massage.

She's pre-occupied, and it only rankles because it concerns me that she's always on.

"Do you want to talk about it?" I ask as I dig into a particularly nasty knot.

"It's Felix Alexander. What he did to Calliope sticks in my craw. Today it became clear that, even if I had been called in, I don't know that there would have been anything I could do. He's insulated himself from this whole business exceptionally well. That doesn't mean I'm not still pissed at Janet for leaving Calliope swinging in the wind. I just hope she doesn't fall all the way down. Meanwhile, I'm watching for Felix to slip up so I can see the look on his face when his world comes crashing down.

"I think it's fair for you to take a little glee when someone purposely fucks up after they've been a piece of shit."

"I don't really need any encouragement—ouch."

"Not sorry. It's the perfect set up—a sadist working out the knots and kinks in his little subbie's back and shoulders."

"Yeah, I guess it almost qualifies as good pain."

"Are you getting hungry?"

"Yeah, actually I am. What would you like?"

"Dinner is already planned. You just need to sit tight here, and I will bring it to you."

I return a few minutes later with the homemade minestrone soup and fresh bread I made this afternoon.

"Oh. My. God. You cooked. Did you bake this bread?"

"Yes, little subbie, I made the bread."

She slathers it in butter, takes a big bite, and lets out long moan, not unlike the sounds she makes when she comes.

"So. Good," she says through her mouthful.

"Weren't you taught that it's rude to talk with your mouth full?"

She just shrugs, dips her bread into the soup and takes another enormous bite.

When we're finished eating, I clear away our dishes and bring us each back another glass of wine.

"Are you in the mood for a movie or a show?" I ask.

"If it's something short. I'm super tired and might fall asleep on you. Talk about scintillating company."

We get most of the way through an episode of *Brooklyn 99* before she flakes out, and I carry her off to bed.

FORTY-ONE

Mel

Stuart has been here for nearly a week and it's been too perfect. When I got called out at three this morning, he didn't complain about being woken up. Instead, he got up and made me coffee to go.

"Text me when you're on your way home," he'd said as he kissed me goodbye.

It took me nearly seven hours to get the situation under control, nearly half of that time was spent calming down my rightfully freaked out client. The other part was spent mostly mediating. All I can say is thank fuck there were no children or animals tangled up in that disaster of a marriage.

By the time I'm done, I'm emotionally drained. I should go to the office, but home is the more appealing option.

Stuart is there.

I admonish myself for being weak and wanting to lean on him for comfort. He's only around for a short time. It would be foolish allow myself to get attached.

When I arrive home, Stuart takes one look at me and hugs me. "Looks like you had a rough morning. I'll go run the water for a bath while you get undressed."

Ten minutes later, I'm in a tub full of hot water and bubbles, leaning back against Stuart's chest while he rubs my shoulders. His erection prods my back, but he just keeps kneading at my knotted muscles.

"Were you able to get back to sleep after I left?" I ask

"I didn't bother trying. I wasn't going to laze around in bed while you were out working. I caught up on my email and had a breakfast video-chat with Ffion after school."

"How's she doing?"

"Typical eleven-year-old stuff. I think there's a boy. She didn't outright say it, but she kind of beat around the bush. I think I'd better come through on a pony. Horse-y girls don't have time for boys."

I chuckle.

Another reason I shouldn't get attached. There is no way I ever want to get in the way of his relationship with her.

"Hey. Where did you just go?" He kisses my temple.

I reach behind me and wrap my fingers around his cock.

Grabbing my wrist, he guides my hand away. "Nope. If you've got stuff going on in your head you don't want to talk about, then you say that. Don't use sex as a distraction.

Busted.

"Still processing my emotions," I hedge.

"Okay." He kisses my temple again and lets me just be.

***

Stuart is flying home tomorrow, and I wanted to take the whole day off and spend it with him. But just after two that afternoon, the universe conspires against me.

"I'm sorry."

"You have nothing to be sorry for. I am not here to disrupt your life. Just to hopefully enhance it a little."

"You do." And after tomorrow he won't.

"Go work your magic, and I'll be right here when you get back."

Except he's not.

Because the bat-shit crazy my client got tangled up in took all fucking night to unravel and by the time I get home, Stuart's already at the airport.

My heart hurts more than I ever thought possible. Like someone has taken a razor blade and sliced out a huge chunk.

I was a fool to let myself get used to having him around.

It's been nearly a month since I last saw Stuart. I've been so overwhelmed with work, I wasn't able to find an opportunity to go to him.

You hear about people lamenting how hard it is to maintain long distance relationships, and it's easy to write that off—they're just not trying hard enough.

Until you're living it.

Phone sex has its place. But it's more effective as a seasoning than a base.

Emotional intimacy is probably the biggest casualty. The loss of nuance in a conversation. Lack of visual cues. Sure, there's video-chat, but even that doesn't have the same effect on a conversation as physically being in the same room.

His flight is due to land any minute and my heart is fluttering against my chest. What if things aren't the same? What if they are? Silly, scary thoughts about what this is between Stuart and me bounce around my head like a pinball.

FORTY-TWO

Stuart

Mel is there waiting when I arrive at the airport. I didn't truly realize how much I've missed her until I have her in my arms.

I kiss her long, and hard and squeeze her tight. "Take me home."

For the entire drive back to her house I'm either holding her hand or stroking her thigh. My need to touch her is insatiable.

As soon as we're through her front door, I drag her off to the bedroom. "Strip. It's been too long since I've had unfettered access to your delectable body, and I won't wait another second."

Once she's naked I pull her into my arms and kiss her silly while I squeeze her ass. "I want to spend this week marking these cheeks up so you'll think of me whenever you sit down."

Moaning, she grinds against my straining erection. "I think someone is horny."

"On your back on the bed, legs spread wide. I need to taste you."

Pushing her thighs wider apart, I nestle in between and nip my way up, stopping just before I reach her glistening pussy.

Her frustrated groan makes my dick harder.

"Patience, love."

I nip my way up the other leg, this time when I reach the top, I take a long, wet swipe of her pussy with my tongue.

"I've missed this, Ms. Seymour." I take another long lick which makes her squirm and moan.

"Louder. I want to hear exactly how much you like this."

Latching my lips over her clit, I flick it with the tip of my tongue, then suck hard and she moans louder. "You may come as much as you can, love."

This time when I return my mouth to her pussy, I slide two fingers deep inside and stroke her g-spot. Her hips buck and I suck harder, flick faster, and piston my fingers inside her.

Her leg shakes and she lets loose a long wail as her orgasm grips her. I keep up the rhythm until I wring out a second and third from her, then kiss my way up her body, taking time to pay special attention to her breasts.

Her nipples are hard and I take one into my mouth, sucking gently as I roll my tongue around it. She rocks her hips, grinding against me.

"Please, Stuart."

I don't correct her. I want this connection. I release her nipple. "What do you want, Mel?"

"You. Naked and inside me. Please."

"As you wish."

After I shuck my clothes, I settle between her legs and notch the tip of my cock to her entrance.

"Ask me again."

"Please fuck me, Stuart."

Taking her mouth in a hot, hungry kiss, I rock my hips forward and slide in deep. I hold myself still inside her, savoring the moment before I take up a slow, steady rhythm. Out to the tip, in to the root, and grind against her clit. All the while, I keep kissing her as though my life depends on it.

Before long, Mel's moans become frantic and I end our kiss. "Please, may I come?"

"As much as you like, love."

I take her lips again, and when she starts to come, I pick up speed, moving faster and harder, holding back my own orgasm until she's come a second time.

I roll sideways and wrap her in my arms. "Hi."

She grins against my left pec. "Hi."

It's on the tip of my tongue to tell her how much I've missed her. To tell her other things, too. But something holds me back. Instead, I just hold her close and bury my face in her hair.

FORTY-THREE

Mel

After a long, sleepless night, I know I need to end it. It's the end of another stolen week and I can't think of any other way forward for me—for us, really—that won't end up with my heart irreparably broken.

"Stuart, we need to talk."

"What's wrong?"

"I can't do this anymore. We need to stop seeing each other."

"Because...?" He lifts his eyebrow and I can feel my resolve weaken slightly.

"While what we have is fun, it isn't sustainable. We both have established careers. You live way the hell up in Canada, and I live here. The best we're managing is a week here and there, and I'm not interested in having a long-distance relationship. It's better to call this done now, before this gets out of hand."

"Out of hand?"

"You know…getting too comfortable." I'm already getting too used to him being here to take care of me when I've had a hard day— I can't afford to rely on that, then have everything go to shit and then it's gone for good.

"Ah, you're concerned we might start having serious feelings for each other."

"I get phone calls at all hours."

"Yes, you do. So do doctors, but they seem to be capable of maintaining relationships."

"Cops, not so much."

He chuckles. "I look on you more as a doctor who fixes things rather than a cop who has to hunt down the bad guy."

Except he's wrong. I'm more like the cop than a doctor. And, probably better he doesn't know that.

"Stuart, I'm being serious, here."

"So am I. I think you're wrong, but I'm not going to argue with you on this right now. I have a plane to catch.

Part of me is a little disappointed that he doesn't fight for us. But I did spend the entire night thinking about this, and really, it was the best solution.

For my heart, anyway.

We spend the next hour while Stuart gets ready to leave in uncomfortable silence, and I hate it. It's not any kind of angry silence, not on my part anyway. More of a don't know what to say kind of silence.

"Are you ready?" I ask. "We should get a move on, in

case traffic is bad." Who am I kidding? Traffic is always bad.

"Yeah. Just let me grab my bag."

The silence continues the entire way to the airport, and I have this overwhelming urge to apologize and ask him to pretend like this morning's conversation never happened.

But I don't.

Because I know in my heart this is the best thing for both of us. I'll carry on doing life the way I did before we met, and he'll find himself a sweet little Canadian sub who'll rock his world into happy ever after.

When I pull into the drop-off area, he leans over and kisses my cheek, removing any question of whether I should get out of the car for a kiss and a hug.

As soon as he shuts the door, I drive away. I can't look at him, let alone wave goodbye.

FORTY-FOUR

Stuart

I'm not surprised when Mel drives off without even saying goodbye. Disappointed, for sure, but not surprised. She may be a great problem solver for the world's rich and famous, but she's kind of sucking at it in her private life.

But, isn't that often the way? People who excel at things for the outside world aren't so capable when it comes to taking care of themselves.

The first thing I do when I walk in the door is head straight to the fridge and grab myself a beer. Okay, so technically it's day-drinking, but I don't drink on airplanes, and I've had a seriously shit day.

I thought we were making the long-distance thing work. Okay, so I did a shit job of tapping into the fact that it wasn't working for her. But that's a two-way street.

Maybe if she'd said something sooner, we could have found a way to make it work for both of us.

Then I start to get a little pissed off. How could it not be working for her, when I was doing most of the travel?

Fuck. I'm a ridiculous mess.

The next morning, I ignore the result of one beer too many last night and mainline coffee as I adjust my schedule. I was going to start on the quickie palate-cleanser project I had lined up to clear my head from the last big one. But I need to keep my mind off Mel. And the only way I'm going to manage that is if I'm focused on something complicated.

And it works. Kind of. As long as I'm working, I'm fine. The problem comes in those off hours. Like eating and sleeping. And showering.

I come up for air nearly a month after I'd returned home. My heart still feels like it's been run through a military grade shredder, and I call the only person I know who could possibly understand.

Ethan answers on the third ring. "How are things with you and Mel?"

I let out a long, heavy sigh. "Done. The long-distance thing was too much."

"Oh man, I'm sorry. But like I told you before, if you're not prepared to give up everything to have her, then she's not for you."

"Thanks for the reminder, Ethan. Exactly what I needed. I hate to cut this short..."

"It's all good. Glad I could help."

After I disconnect the call, I think about what exactly I'd be giving up by moving. Ffion? I've seen her maybe once since I got home. She's more into texting and video-chatting these days.

Work? I can set up to do that anywhere.

My house? I can keep it. It's not like I'm moving to outer Siberia. It's less than a three-hour direct flight.

My mood perks as the beginnings of a plan come together.

FORTY-FIVE

Mel

It's been six lonely weeks since I sent Stuart packing back up to Canada. The longest we've been apart since Fetwrk went live. I know it was for the best, even if my heart disagrees.

My assistant's voice over the intercom pulls me from my thoughts. "Mel, Eli Simmons is here to see you."

"You can send him in."

Seconds later, there's a staccato knock on my door before it opens.

"Eli, come on in, have a seat. Can I get you coffee or something?"

"No, thanks. I'm good. What did you want to see me about?"

"I'm cautiously optimistic that Tara Langston will no longer be a problem. However, if she shows up in your life in any way, you're to let me know immediately so I can take steps. Understood?"

"Got it."

"Excellent. Now, if you're looking to get down and kinky, there is now a safer way to do it. Do you know how to install apps on your phone that don't come from an app store?"

"Uh, no."

I stand and take the seat next to him on the other side of my desk.

"Unlock your phone, and I'll show you. In case, for any reason you need to reinstall."

A few minutes later, I have Fetwrk installed on his phone.

"There. You can set up your account in private when you've got a good chunk of free time. An hour or two at least so you can give it your full attention. The more accurate your information, the better your matches will be."

"How do I know the person I connect with isn't going to turn out to be another Tara? Or worse?"

"Access to this app is restricted to high-profile public figures. It's mutually assured destruction. Outing you would out themselves, so they have everything to lose and nothing to gain. That said, there are some fail-safes in place. While users can use any screen name they like, the app has access through their phone to their identity and contact info which is kept securely on the back-end. I don't understand the nitty-gritty of how it all works, I just know that if there is a real problem, we have access to real life identities."

"Okay. So, what happens after I get all my information loaded into the app?"

"It's like Tinder or any of those other hook-up apps, for the most part. There's a match percentage threshold that you can set. So, maybe you're only interested in hooking up with people who are a ninety-percent match, then the app will only notify you of potential partners who meet or exceed that threshold. Of course, the higher you set the threshold, the fewer available options you'll have. So, you'll probably want to find a threshold that will maximize the number of compatible partners, but still allow that neither of you need to compromise so much that a good time isn't had by all."

"Do you have a recommended threshold?"

"No. I'm afraid it's a bit of hit and miss until you find it. Everyone is too different for me to be able to give a generic starting point. Spend some time with the app. I think once you've completed the account set up, you'll have a general sense of what your threshold might be. You can alter it anytime and as often as you like. So, one day, you might be feeling a little more flexible and lower your threshold, another day, you might find you need to connect with someone more in tune with your own needs. Any more questions?"

"Not right now."

As soon as Eli leaves, I go home.

FORTY-SIX

Stuart

While there are still a lot of arrangements left to be made before my move is complete, three months after Mel pushed me away, I've settled into a life here in L.A. I'm ready to see if Mel is willing to give things another shot.

"Hi Stuart," Christine greets me with a wide grin as I enter the main reception area of Mel's office. "How are you today?"

"I'm fabulous, how about you?"

"Pretty good. Mel should be finished any minute. Have a seat, and I'll just go ahead and clear her schedule for the rest of the day."

"Thank you."

I'm only waiting ten minutes when Christine ushers me through. "I was able to clear her schedule until tomorrow after lunch," she says with a wink.

I give a quick knock on the door, then let myself in. "Delivery for Mel Seymour."

She looks up and grins for a moment, before wiping her face of all expression.

"Stuart. What are you doing here? I told you—"

"I know what you told me. You said you weren't interested in having a long-distance relationship. I'm not either, so I've been busy removing that barrier to our happiness."

I hand over the roll of papers I've tied with a purple ribbon. "I've brought you a present."

She undoes the ribbon and unfurls the documents, her eyes scanning the pages at lighting speed. Then she looks up at me.

"You had Wil perform a background check?"

"Yes."

"You do realize I had him perform one before I hired you to design Fetwrk, right?"

"He told me as much. But I wanted you to have the most up-to-date version."

"Why?"

"No secrets. Well, except of the governmental top sort."

"You've moved here?"

"Of course."

"What about your house in Vancouver?"

"Home base for you and me whenever we're there. I do like the house, and it's nicer than having to stay in a hotel, don't you think? Also, not many hotels equipped with a dungeon for when the mood to kink strikes."

"You're sure about this?"

"Mel, I love you. You are the most important person in the world to me. These past three months without you have been lonely and miserable, and none of that changed until I accepted the truth and did everything necessary to move closer to you."

"You didn't buy a house, did you? Because that would be ridiculous when—"

"I'm currently renting. You're not ready for cohabitation yet. But when you are, then we'll discuss our living arrangements."

"It's a ridiculous waste of money for you to rent when I have plenty of room in my perfectly good house."

"Mel, we've taken a number of aspects of our relationship a little on the fast side. Living together is a big step, and I don't want you to feel rushed, or pushed. We'll know when it's time. Until then, I still expect to share a bed every night whenever we're both in the same city. We'll just maintain our own space."

She looks at her watch and I chuckle. "Christine cleared your schedule. You're off the clock until tomorrow morning. Want to go get some lunch?"

"I'd rather you take me home."

FORTY-SEVEN

Mel

I can't believe Stuart just up and left his life to relocate here, with me. The idea of it is so overwhelming. And until I met him, it's something I could never have imagined myself doing.

Yet, not that long ago, I started toying with the idea, myself. I even went so far as to assess the feasibility of me moving my business holdings to Vancouver. The realities of what that would entail were more than I could wrap my head around.

Meanwhile, Stuart just turned around and did exactly that.

Don't go there. Think of something else

Like an office in Vancouver. Yeah, that might merit a little more consideration. Perhaps one in London, too.

"Where did you just go, Mel?"

"I was just thinking about opening a Vancouver office."

He cocks an eyebrow. "Oh, really?"

"Well, before you showed up, making your grand gesture this morning, I had already been thinking about how I could swing moving up north. Would you have preferred that?"

"No. I wouldn't ever want you to rearrange your life around me."

"Yet you did exactly that. What makes it okay for you, but not me?"

"My work isn't location dependent in the same way yours is. And no matter how you look at it, L.A. is the place where most of the work is that only you can do. Even if you had a private jet at your disposal, you'd still be hours away from a first response to a scandal if you were based in Vancouver. And besides, I'm here now. It's done. If you decide to set up satellite offices in other cities because it makes good business sense, then I'm all for that. But, for now, I believe it's in *your* best business interest to be located here. And I would be surprised if you didn't agree with me."

"You're right. But what about Ffion?"

"Ffion is old enough to fly unaccompanied. She can come visit.

The sheer magnitude of what he did hits me full in the chest.

And I realize that regardless of the hurdles, if he hadn't come to me, I would have gone to him.

Eventually.

I stare at him for a second. "I love you, Stuart." The words tumble out because my feelings for him are so big, I just can't hold them in any longer.

I don't *want* to hold them in any longer. "More than I ever thought possible."

He wraps his arms around me and holds me tight, making those feelings I have a little less scary. "I love you, too, sweetheart. Wherever you are, is home to me."

"Besides," He plants a loud, smacking kiss on my forehead. "not having your cute little ass close by for me to whale on whenever the mood strikes made me grumpy."

"Funny, you not being close enough for you to whale on my ass made me grumpy, too."

"Perhaps we should do something about that, then. Skirt up, panties to your knees, and bend over the end of the bed, little subbie."

The jangle of his belt unbuckling and the whisper of the leather sliding through the loops of his jeans makes my belly quiver in anticipation as I wait for the first strike across my unmarked flesh.

"Such a lovely blank canvas. I will enjoy leaving my marks on it. Ten to start, I think, because I'm pretty sure that's about as many as I can manage before the need to be inside you is too much for me to bear."

I hear the swish of the belt cutting through the air a nano-second before the leather strikes my skin. It's been so long since I've had a spanking of any sort, my skin is re-sensitized to the pain. He takes no breaks between swings, and before long, I'm flying.

"Such a good girl for me, Mel. I missed you so much."

"I missed you too, Sir. I'm sorry I sent you away."

"Sweetheart, it's okay. You did what you needed to do, and as it turned out, it was what I needed for you to do, too. In the end, it's working out just fine for both of us.

EPILOGUE

Mel

Two years later

It never ceases to amaze me how quickly and easily Stuart uprooted himself and made his place in my life, I think to myself as I gaze at the man sleeping next to me.

His eyes flutter open, and he's quick to grin when he catches me watching him.

"Good morning, little subbie." Dragging the quilt down to his thighs, he tangles his fingers in my hair and pushes me towards his morning erection. "The sooner you take care of that, the sooner you get coffee."

Parting my lips, I open my throat and take him deep, swallowing against the tip of his cock as he presses me down farther.

"Take it all, little subbie. Hard and fast. I'm in no mood for teasing."

Using both hands, he pulls me off him slightly, then forces me down to the root. With brutal upward hip thrusts, he gains those last precious millimeters, ensuring I take every last bit of his cock. Even though my gag reflex is mostly gone, the pressure when he does this always makes my gut give a little lurch. Which, of course, is exactly why he does it.

"Yes, baby, that's it."

He pulls me up, and I swirl around the head with my tongue until he pushes me back down again.

Up, swirl, down, thrusts, lurch, repeat.

It's not long before I feel the tell-tale swell of his shaft.

"Be a good girl and swallow it all," he tells me, needlessly, as he sends spurt after spurt of semen down my throat.

When he's done, I gently lick him clean. He's supersensitive after he comes. Kind of like my clit can be, especially after a long session of forced orgasms. And sometimes, when I'm feeling bratty, I *accidentally* lick a little too hard and make him flinch. He makes me pay for it later. Which is exactly why I do it. Yeah, so that might be a little bit of topping from the bottom, but it works for us, so who cares?

"Such a good girl for me. Give me a minute to recover, and I'll go make you coffee."

I rest my head on his chest and listen to his heartbeat. It's my favorite sound. Well, that and the noise he makes when he comes. The first is my peace. The second is my power.

I half wake up when he kisses my temple and slides out of bed. "Go back to sleep. I'll be back with your coffee soon."

The next thing I know, there's an annoying, persistent tickling at my ear. I try to bat it away, but I miss, and it keeps coming back. It's the sharp nip that brings me fully awake and protesting.

"You're mean," I tell Stuart. He just chuckles and pulls me in for a hug.

"You wouldn't want me any other way."

"True enough."

"I have an important question to ask you."

"Before coffee?"

"Yes, before coffee."

"Is me getting coffee dependent on this answer?"

"Nope."

"Can I at least have a sip of my coffee first?"

"Nope. And the longer you persist with this futile attempt at negotiation, the longer you'll wait for your coffee."

"Fine."

He takes my hand and kisses each knuckle. "Mel. I love you, and I want to spend my life with you. Will you marry me and wear my collar?"

I'd hoped it would come to this. Fantasized about it. But no matter how good my imagination is, I'm not ready for the depth of emotion his question evokes.

My heart all but explodes with the knowledge that he wants to spend his life with me. That after two years and all my oddities, he wants me enough to make it official. "Yes. A thousand times, yes."

He slides his hand behind my head and pulls me in for a deep, greedy kiss.

"You've made me the happiest man alive. I know I should have probably had a ring ready, but I wanted us to choose it together. Yes, there will times when I take control and make the decisions, just as I've always done, but when it comes to your rings, that's a symbol of our partnership, and something we will do together. When it comes to your collar, however…I'll need to think on that."

"Can I have my coffee now, please, Sir?"

He grabs my mug off his nightstand and hands it to me.

I take my first sip, and as always, it tastes of pure love.

THE END

ACKNOWLEDGMENTS

Jean Siska for answering legal questions. Anything I got wrong is 100% on me because I'm perfectly happy to bastardise reality if it gets in the way of the story.

Zoe York for insisting Mel needed to have her own story rather than be a prologue and also for the beautiful covers.

Tymber Dalton, for brainstorming, hand holding, and the wicked predicament bondage scenario.

Susan Hayes for talking me off ledges and being just a few hours away.

My editor, Dayna Hart for being kind and gentle, but always straight with me. Also for handling my editing emergencies—and they're all emergencies.

Vera and Nancy for the emergency beta-reads.

And always, Math-geek, who puts up with crazy deadline me with very little complaint.

ABOUT THE AUTHOR

Surrounded by mist-covered mountains, Sadie Haller lives a quiet life with her husband and fur-babies.

Where to find Sadie
sadiehaller.com
sadie@sadiehaller.com
Follow on Bookbub

www.ingramcontent.com/pod-product-compliance
Lightning Source LLC
Chambersburg PA
CBHW010510100726
47902CB00011B/2158